Lady Atkins

The Hermit

Vol. 1

Lady Atkins

The Hermit
Vol. 1

ISBN/EAN: 9783337048181

Printed in Europe, USA, Canada, Australia, Japan

Cover: Foto ©Andreas Hilbeck / pixelio.de

More available books at **www.hansebooks.com**

THE
HERMIT.

A NOVEL.

By A LADY. ATKINS

IN TWO VOLUMES.

VOL. I.

LONDON:

Printed for H. GARDNER, oppofite St. Clement's
Church, Strand; and fold by J. WALTER,
at Charing-Crofs; and G. PEARCH,
at No. 12, in Cheapfide.

MDCCLXIX.

THE

H E R M I T.

CHAP. I.

BOUT forty miles from the Metropolis is a village, for beauty out-vying the many delightful ones with which this island abounds. — Verdant fields, enamelled with flowers, are here made ftill more charming by a ferpentine river that meanders through them. —Upon the velvet margin of this clair mirror the lovely nymph may contemplate her dazzling complexion, without fear of having it injured by the scorching sun; nature having planted its banks so thick with elms, limes, and willows, that though *Phœbus*, in his journey, now and then gives them a glance, yet his rays are so mild that the most celebrated belle would not have run from them.

THIS walk was to our rural lads and lasses what the *Mall* or *Green-park* are to those of a more exalted sphere.

HERE every new gown or cap was shewn for the first time.—It was here *Amintor* got the blushing *Sylvia* to declare she preferred him to *Cimon*;— for, as the damsel rightly observed, What are great riches without the man one loves? and, to prove these were her real sentiments, she determined never

ver more to see the opulent *Cimon*, who was then in actual possession of a mill and two acres of ground.—It was here too, in this very walk, that *Roger* swore he would be constant to his dear *Susan*; who, in return, protested she had sooner three of Sir *Francis Gilford*'s best cows should die, than that *Tom* the footman should again touch her hand.

After such an assurance, could he have any doubt of his *Susan*'s faith, she being dairy-maid to the Baronet, and, it was thought, loved her *keey* better than any other earthly thing, except honest *Roger*.

Sir *Francis Gilford* being at this time the *Goliath*, or, in other words, head man in the village, it will be necessary to give my reader a sketch of

the

the family at the *Grange*, that being
the name of the feat in which the
Gilfords had refided for a century
paft.

CHAP. II.

SIR *Gregory*, father of the prefent
incumbent, was, in every fenfe of
the word, an honeft man; that is, a
good hufband, — a tender parent, — a
fincere friend,—a kind landlord.

These were his characteriftics. His
income, though large, was fcarce fufficient for his unbounded generofity.
The worthy and friendlefs were always fure of a welcome at his table.
The indigent, that continually crouded
his gates, went not away unfatisfied.
Never was forrow fo contagious as at
the

the little parish of *Weatly*, when death
took from them their patron and bene-
factor.

LADY *Gilford* wanted her husband's
nobleness of soul ; but nothing of this
deficiency appeared whilst he lived. Her
actions might be said to shine through
his ; nor was her heart unlike those flowers which expand their foliage to the sun,
but no sooner is its congenial influence
withdrawn, than it again sinks into its
native littleness ; so was her mind for
a time enlarged by the example of her
husband, but having lost that, became
narrow and contracted.

AFTER the interment of Sir *Gregory*,
Hospitality, which in the lifetime of
that good man always stood as Porter,
was immediately discharged, and his
place supplied by Parsimony. As the

former

former by fmiles and affability invited
all to enter; fo the meagre and four vi-
fage of the latter kept them out as ef-
fectually as bolts and bars.

It was by means of this new fervant that the prefent heir poffeffes an
eftate clearing fix thoufand *per annum,*
which at his father's death hardly
amounted to five; yet he could not
properly be faid to gain by this acqui-
fition, as it was procured him at the ex-
pence of the moft profound ignorance
in all that is learned or polite.

In the place of *Homer*, *Horace*,
and *Virgil*, he fubftituted fuch authors
as could beft inform him in the rife
and fall of ftock, or inftruct him in the
true value of land; in which he made fo
fwift a progrefs, that after an exact cal-
culation he found it was ftill poffible to
raife

raife his eftates five hundred annually: this he determined to do by turning out thofe old tenants of his father's who would not come into his terms.

THE joyful mother's eyes fparkled with pleafure to fee the happy bent of her fon's difpofition; fhe felt no fears on his account, having moulded his heart according to her own fordid principles: it had often paffed the ordeal trial, by being expofed to the moft diftreffed objects; but, always to the great fatisfaction of Lady *Gilford*, was hardened by the fight.

Though mild-eyed Pity was banifhed by a wrong-judging parent from the breaft of Sir *Francis*, it was not unmindful of the warm reception it had formerly met with in that of his father; for which reafon, unwilling to

leave

leave a family where he had been once
so diftinguifhed, he fhook his dove-
like pinions, and flew for fhelter to the
bofom of *Lavinia*; which finding to
be alfo a habitation for the Virtues and
the Graces, determined from that inftant to make it his abode.　To fpeak
without a metaphor, never were difpo-
fitions more diametrically oppofite than
this brother and fifter.

OFTEN with inexpreffible concern
had this amiable girl feen and fhed
tears at the inftances of unfeeling inhu-
manity that peeped out in all his actions, yet fhe never difputed with him.
She would fay to herfelf, " If dead to
" the pleading of compaffion, will any
" thing that I can urge affect him?"
ftriving by her own benevolence to
prevent, as much as fhe could do, the
cruelty he meditated.

YET

YET in this she was obliged to follow closely the rule prescribed us in the Scriptures, Not to let our left hand know what our right hand doeth; for had any of these acts of generosity, which constituted the sole delight of *Lavinia*, come to the ears of Lady *Gilford*, she would have been sure to have fallen under her Ladyship's severe displeasure. Indeed, she had never been a favourite of her mother, whose whole stock of fondness was lavished on Sir *Francis*; nor is this partiality to be wondered at, there being in their sentiments so strict a unity.

AT the commencement of this History, Miss *Gilford* had gained her twentieth year, the first seventeen of which had fled away with a pleasing rapidity: but it was not so with the last three; they had dragged heavily on,

as if upon their wing they bore the
troubles which had rent her tender
heart : yet to make her fome requital,
they brought to *Weatly*, about fix
months before this period, Mr. *Coventry* and his daughter, in whofe converfation *Lavinia* found fuch pleafure,
that in thofe hours fpent at *Hartly-row*
fhe almoft forgot to think herfelf unhappy.

As my readers are unacquainted with
this little family, I muft ftep back to
their firft arrival, or rather to a fketch
of their hiftory before that time ; but
thinking it is a poor compliment to in-
troduce people of their merit at the end
of a chapter, I fhall dedicate another to
that purpofe.

CHAP. III.

IT being a received opinion, that the Feminine gives precedency to the Masculine, we shall for that reason beg Miss *Coventry*'s pardon a few minutes to bring the reader acquainted with her worthy father.

MR. *Coventry* was a man both of family and fortune, had received a liberal education, extremely sensible, with a thorough knowledge of men and manners.—He made what is called the Grand Tour, but did not return so heavy laden as many of our *British* youth, being curious to cull none but flowers: as for weeds, he was of opinion we had already too many of our own growth.

BEFORE

Before the age of twenty-five he had visited most of the courts in *Europe*, at none of which he passed unnoticed. A certain great Potentate, of whom he was a particular favourite, would have detained him at ————; but that not suiting with his plan, he declined the Monarch's intended favour, tho' with such modesty and gratitude, that his Majesty honoured him with letters to the *French* Court, wherein he was mentioned in such high terms as occasioned a contest who should distinguish himself most, by shewing civilities to the favourite of so great a prince.

The death of his father hastened his return to *England*, where he soon after married Miss *Villers*, a young lady of great merit but small fortune, to whom his affections had been long engaged;

engaged; yet as the alliance was not agreeable to his father, Mr. *Coventry* determined to facrifice his Love to his Duty; nor would his honour fuffer him even to hint a defire to the lady, of keeping her heart referved till he mig...... be at liberty to offer her his own in exchange.

NEVER had he openly declared his paffion; and dreading to fee that hand beftowed on another which would have made him happy, he refolved for fome years to leave *England*.

EVERY thing being fettled for his departure, he went to pay a laft vifit to Mifs *Villers*, whom he acquainted with his defign.— A tear, which could not be fuppreffed, efcaped her; yet by words fhe did not attempt to detain him.— They parted.—He fet out the next day

on

on his travels, whilst she retired to the
confolatory arms of an indulgent aunt
who lived at *Weatly*, both fecretly in
love with each other, and both determined never to marry, if Fate should
deny them the object of their wishes.

THEIR conftancy was not put to a
long trial; death thought fit to call on
the elder Mr. *Coventry* two years after
his fon left *England*; on which event
he returned: and no obftacle now remaining to his union with Mifs *Villers*,
they interchanged their mutual vows
at the altar.

THE ceremony being performed at
Weatly, in compliance with the intreaties of their aunt *Prefton*, they ftill continued her vifitors. The fituation of this
fweet place had fomething in it fo
very pleafing, the happinefs they there

en-

enjoyed was fo exquifite, that they fcarce ever thought of returning into what is called the Great World.

AMBITION often courts thofe to whom he is moft obnoxious; at leaft it was now the cafe with Mr. *Coventry.* Lord *L——*, a man in great power, and his coufin-german, well knew how very fit this relation was to fupport the character for which he had deftined him.

AN ambaffador was to be fent to the court of ——, when his Lordfhip propofed Mr. *Coventry,* who was ac‑ cordingly nominated.

As men are apt to judge of others fentiments by their own, Lord *L*—— thought fuch an honour could not avoid giving his coufin the higheft
plea‑

pleafure; for which reafon a meffenger was difpatched to acquaint him with it; at the fame time defiring his immediate attendance. Mr. *Coventry* and his Lady received this mandate in a far different manner than was expected by their noble kinfman; their hearts were fo intirely filled with Love, that Ambition could not find fo much as a corner to inhabit.

However, he determined to accept the embaffy; but without a view either to honour or profit.—It was the pleafure of his Monarch that he fhould go, and this alone at once refolved him; on which he wrote a polite letter to Lord *L——*, thanking that nobleman, and fignifying his defign of coming to town the next week.

Mrs.

Mrs. *Coventry* determining to accompany her hufband, they took a tender leave of Mrs. *Prefton*, and fet out for the Metropolis.——His credentials were foon ready ; they embarked, and after a fhort delightful voyage arrived fafe at ———. Formerly he had refided fome months at this court, and was again received with particular marks of efteem.

Mrs. *Coventry* met with univerfal admiration ; nor is it to be wondered at, as fhe furpaffed almoft every woman in external as well as internal beauties.

This confeffed fuperiority did not excite the leaft fpirit of envy ; emulation was the only paffion fhe infpired in the breafts of thofe fair dames.

BALLS,

BALLS, Concerts, Mafquerades had flown away with twelve months, when Mr. *Coventry* received orders to return immediately to *England*, but not till he had declared war with ——— : fuch a command as this he had but little reafon to expect, as our court and that of —— were at this time feemingly on the moft amicable terms.

HAVING no defign to dive into the political caufes for this war, or why Mr. *Coventry* had not been made fooner acquainted with them, I fhall only fay he did as he was directed by his late order.

AFTER taking a polite leave, he embarked with his Lady, though her going was entirely againft the advice of the learned, as fhe was very near the time of her delivery.

EVEN

EVEN Mr. *Coventry* ufed every per-
fuafion to make her continue at ———
till fhe was delivered.—No arguments
could prevail, and they embarked together.

IT is a common and juft obferva-
tion, That love will fometimes make
a coward of the braveft.

MR. *Coventry* had never till now
known what it was to fear.—Winds
had blown from every point: he had,
as the Royal Pfalmift elegantly de-
fcribes it, " feen the fea mount to the
heavens, and return with equal impe-
tuofity to the nethermoft deep," yet his
mind continued unmoved:—but now
the time was come when his foul
feemed ruffled by every breath of air.
—If the weather was fair, he dreaded
a calm :

a calm:—again, if it blew frefh, a ftorm would certainly enfue.—Whole hours would he even deprive himfelf of his Lady's company to walk on the deck, contemplating the hemifphere: ten times in an hour would he afk the failors if the winds continued favourable.

Mrs. *Coventry* on her part, fhewed much more heroifm.

She faw her hufband's anxiety, and knew it was on her account; fhe therefore exerted her refolution, which nothing elfe could have made her exert; for a natural dread of the water, joined to an extreme ficknefs, made her fuffer a great deal: however, at length they were both relieved by being fafely landed at *Dover*.

HAVING

HAVING once more feen them fet foot on *terra firma*, we think it high time to put an end to the chapter.

****

CHAP. IV.

A Few hours after they difembarked they proceeded to *London*, a houfe in *Great Ormond-Street* being provided for their reception.

THE next morning Mr. *Coventry* waited on his Majefty, by whom he was moft gracioufly received; and ftaying only a fhort time at St. *James's*, paid a vifit to Lord *L——*. It was by his Lordfhip he was made acquainted with the reafons for his fudden recall to *England*; but as that gentleman defired them to be kept a profound fe-cret,

cret, I do not think myfelf at liberty to difclofe of what nature they were.

We muft now leave him with his Lordſhip, and return to Mrs. *Coventry,* who, though far from well when her huſband left her, yet had made no complaint; but now found it would be foon neceſſary to fend for Mrs. *D——*; and in a few hours a meſſage was difpatched to Mr. *Coventry* to acquaint him his Lady was fafely delivered of a daughter.

Can my reader form any idea of the joy a poor wretch receives, who having but ten pounds ventures his little all in the lottery; if it turns out a blank he ſtarves, and when his hopes are at the loweft ebb up comes the ten thoufand:—or fuppofe the tranfports of a man who receives a reprieve juft as the dreaded mufquets are levelled at his head:—if he can raife to himfelf any picture of fuch fenfations, then may he in fome meafure judge of Mr. *Coventry*'s.

HE handfomely rewarded the perfon who brought him the intelligence; and flinging himfelf into his chariot, ordered to be drove home with great expedition.

THE way from *Hanover-Square* to *Ormond-Street* not being a great length, and the horfes appearing to have caught fome of their mafter's impatience, he foon faw the welcome door.

THE fervant who opened it did not wear a face of joy: the houfe-keeper, who

who met him in the veſtibule, had
melancholy viſibly painted on her's;
however, it paſſed unnoticed by Mr.
Coventry. People happy in themſelves
are not the firſt to mark the appearance
of misfortunes in others.

WHEN he eagerly enquired after
his Lady, and was informed Doctor
Edgcome would wait on him, without
receiving any other anſwer he began
to be alarmed.

" DOCTOR *Edgcome !* (repeated he)
" For heaven's ſake, Mrs. *Dayly*, what
" can all this mean ! Cannot you an-
" ſwer me ? Is your Lady———."

HE was proceeding; but happening
to glance his eye towards her's, " O
" my God ! (he exclaimed) why thoſe
" tears ? But ſpeak ! ſpeak ! your ſilence
" is,

" is, if poffible, more dreadful than " my own thoughts!"

STILL Mrs. *Dayly* was filent, reply-ing only with her tears: at length fhe pronounced with difficulty, " My " Lady! my Lady, Sir!" and again her voice was choaked.

THIS was enough: he fuddenly dropped upon his knees, he lifted his ftreaming eyes to heaven, and cried out, " Spare, oh gracious God! if " it be thy bleffed will"——the life of my dear wife, he would have faid, but fobs prevented more.

THE Chaplain, who now entered, judged by his pofture and tears, which ftill flowed, that already he was ac-quainted with what he fo much dreaded to inform him; therefore taking him by the hand as foon as he arofe, " Now

" is

" is the time (faid he) my dear Mr.
" *Coventry*, to fhew both the Chriftian
" and the Hero."

" Then fhe is gone! gone for ever!
" (exclaimed he) but tell me, my
" friend,—nor fear my refignation to
" the divine will."

" A heart like yours (replied that
" gentleman) will always think and
" act as it ought.—We fhould not fet
" our minds too much on any thing
" here below.—Mrs. *Coventry*, whilft
" on earth, lived the life of an Angel;
" do not then repine that fhe has now
" for ever joined thofe Bleffed Spirits.
" This is a trial fent you from the
" Almighty;—bear it you muft;—
" therefore, fince it is unavoidable, bear
" it like a Man;—one who hopes to
" meet her again where you will never
" more be difunited."

This

THIS being a favourite topic with the good man, he would probably have carried it much farther, if the fudden fall of Mr. *Coventry* had not interrupted him.

HIS fortitude was not equal to his refignation; for no fooner did he hear fhe was really dead, than his eyefight forfook him, and he fell fenfelefs on the floor.

DOCTOR *Edgcome* was much a-larmed; he rang the bell, and the fervants foon came to his affiftance. Mr. *Coventry* was immediately conveyed to bed, where his recovery was for a long time doubtful.

HOWEVER, the apprehenfions of his friend were at length removed; but a phyfician, who was called in,

ftill

ftill thought him in great danger from the fever into which this fhock had thrown him.

WHOEVER are folicitous for the recovery of this worthy unfortunate gentleman, may receive the gratification of their wifhes in the following chapter.

C H A P. V.

READERS,—if any of you are of the fame way of thinking with the Wife Man, who fays " it is bet-" ter to go to the houfe of mourning " than to the houfe of mirth ;" if any fuch there are amongft you, I not only permit, but alfo invite you to ftay fome

little

little time longer in *Ormond-Street*, where you shall behold real sorrow ; not such as Lady *R*—— expressed for the loss of her Lord ; nor does it bear the least similitude to *Jack Hampton*'s, when, by the death of his elder brother, he came to the title and estate.

MR. *Coventry*'s tears flowed not through the channel either of fashion, custom, or hypocrisy ; they came directly from a heart where the image of his deceased wife afforded them a continual source ; yet time, that kind healer of woes, with the presence of the little *Maria* in some degree stopped their current, and calmed, if not suppressed his afflictions.

MARIA was, at least in his opinion, the exact resemblance of her dear mother. Often would he sit and gaze

whole

whole hours on the miniature, and contemplate her growing charms, which
every day received improvement from
the hand of Time, that feemed refolved to ripen fo fair a bloffom, and
bring it to perfection, that the root
from which it fprung might not fink
into oblivion.

MR. *Coventry* faw the beauties
of his daughter; he faw them with
fatisfaction, with delight, but not without reflection. He rightly judged that
an edifice, though ever fo richly de-
corated by the artift's hand, foon comes
to decay; his chief care, therefore,
was to fit up the apartments of her
foul, not only as they were more dura-
ble, but more worthy of his care.

THE cardinal Virtues he placed
neareft her heart: Affability, Generofity,

fity, and Humanity, with a thoufand other namelefs ones, were ranged by him in fuch beautiful order, that I can only fay, in one word, in mind and perfon *Maria* was the mafter-piece of Nature.

SHE had now attained her fifteenth year, in which time her father's fondnefs had never fuffered her to be fron him ; yet he took care not to let her feel this partiality to her difadvantage.

MASTERS of all kinds had been procured to teach her the polite languages, whilft a governefs was provided to inftruct her in thofe accomplifhments young ladies of fafhion are expected to poffefs.

MR. *Coventry*, though much againft his inclinations, ftayed in town till

Maria was sixteen, when he propoſed once more to viſit the dear ſpot where he had paſſed ſo many hours of felicity with his beloved wife.

Only one diſagreeable circumſtance could attend his removing to *Weatly*. He knew his daughter's duty would not oppoſe any plan of life he approved; but was he ſure her heart would chearfully acquieſce to leave the *beau-monde*, and that general admiration ſhe was ſure to inſpire, whereever ſhe appeared? This reflection gave him uneaſineſs; and nothing but an inclination for retirement, which he could not conquer, would have made him propoſe it to her.

How agreeably was he ſurpriſed to hear his ſweet *Maria* declare, on his firſt hinting it, that nothing could poſſibly
make

make her more happy than such a retirement as he described!

" WE shall there, my dear Sir,
" (said she) find people who will tell
" us their true sentiments without
" flattery: sincerity and friendship are
" surely confined to those charming
" rural retreats."

MR. *Coventry* did not think exactly
with his daughter, yet made no dis-
couraging reply, unwilling to deaden
the rapture with which she embraced
his proposal: however, he knew too
much of mankind to suppose the
Virtues had taken up their resi-
dence in any particular spot, knowing
they were dispersed abroad; and that
whoever are willing to entertain them,
whether in a public circle or a private
shade, whether in a court or cottage,

C 5   may

may always find them ready for admittance.

ABOUT fix weeks after this refolution, Mr. and Mifs *Coventry* took a genteel leave of their general acquaintance, and an affectionate one of Lord *L*——, who was really a worthy man, and had fhewn himfelf their fincere friend on all occafions.

ACCOMPANIED by doctor *Edgcome*, they left *London*, and without any accident or adventure worth relating, arrived fafe at *Weatly*.

HAD Mr. *Coventry* confulted only his own inclinations, he would have declined any acquaintance with the families who had alfo made that their place of refidence; not out of any diflike to them, but a thorough difre-

lifh of company: yet, for *Maria's*
fake, he encouraged thofe advances
that were made, and feldom a day
paffed without their receiving vifits.

Miss *Coventry's* charms were echoed
from all mouths, and in enumerating
them they had not forgot to mention
her fortune.

FIFTY thoufand pounds, and fuch
a lovely girl, could not fail to turn the
heads of all the young fellows of
fafhion in or about *Weatly*.—Her appearance at church the *Sunday* after
their arrival, gained her the hearts of
the whole village, from the lofty baronet down to the fpruce attorney.—
Thofe who had either mother or fifter,
intreated they would by fome means or
other make an acquaintance at *Hartly-
Row*.

THE

THE heart of Sir *Francis Gilford*, which was imagined till now to be made intirely of flint, was, to the furprize of all, but to none more than his mother, found to have in it fomething of a combuftible nature; for it was moft certain his confumed with the multitude.

HER Ladyfhip and her amiable daughter felt great pleafure at this unlooked-for event, though from very different motives.——His fifter, who well knew the effects of that paffion, hoped its influence would humanize his foul, and foften his bear-like temper : yet if it had not this defired power, fhe fincerely wifhed he might not fucceed, as it was impoffible for a man of his difpofition to make happy one fo mild and gentle as Mifs *Coventry* was reported to be.

LADY

LADY *Gilford* confidered nothing but the fortune fhe would bring into her family, which anfwering her moft fanguine expeftations, fhe congratulated Sir *Francis* on his choice; and a card was inftantly difpatched to inform Mr. and Mifs *Coventry*, that, if agreeable, they would wait on them the next afternoon.

A POLITE and fatisfactory anfwer being received to this little billet, I fhall leave them to confult on the important article of drefs, and clofe the chapter.

C H A P.

CHAP. VI.

SIR *Francis*, though mighty plain in his common appearance, would, on this extraordinary occafion, have dreffed himfelf to the beft advantage: but alas! in what a dilemma do we find him? without fo much as a trimmed coat or bag-wig to appear in before his miftrefs.

AT length it occurred to him that he had never vifited his late father's wardrobe, which might poffibly afford him fome relief in this moment of exigency. He flew to his mother, demanded the keys, and haftened thither with more impatience than I can well defcribe.

HAVING

HAVING rummaged over and over every drawer, every box, every trunk, being diftracted in his choice amidft more finery than he expected to meet with, at length he laid his hands on a rich fuit that feemed, as they lay in folds, to pleafe him mightily; and pulling them out from under a heap of other things, equipped himfelf on the fpot, and then went down to have his mother's opinion of his choice.

LADY *Gilford*, when fhe faw him enter her room, cryed out, furveying him from top to toe, " This muft do, " my dear, this muft do, or Mifs *Co-* " *ventry* will not think as I did: the " firft time Sir *Gregory* came to vifit " me in thefe very cloaths, I thought " him the moft graceful figure I " had ever beheld. There is magic " in thefe cloaths,——Ah *Frank!*
" there

" there will be no withstanding you.
" Miss *Coventry* will soon put you in
" possession of her thousands."

THE vain fellow smiled a look of
assent, and fixing his long unmeaning
eyes on an opposite glass, replied;
" Indeed, Madam, I must confess
" your son makes no despicable figure:
" — I think I am tolerable.—I think
" I am not an object to be refused ;—
" I think I am not—Yet damn these
" women, my Lady; there is no an-
" swering for their capricious humours."

" BUT, my dear, (added her Lady-
" ship) your father had a very pretty
" sword, wig, and stockings, that,
" poor man, he always used to wear
" with this suit ; I fancy you may find
" them, and then your dress will be
" complete."

AWAY

AWAY went Sir *Francis* in purfuit of thefe valuable acquifitions; and having been fuccefsful in his fearch, when the coach drew up to the door which was to convey them to Mr. *Coventry's,* he offered his hand to help in the ladies, one of whom could hardly refrain from an immoderate fit of laughter, this being *Lavinia's* firft interview with her wife brother, fince he became a beau of the laft age.

That my Readers may not accufe Mifs *Gilford* of laughing at her own folly, I muft in juftice exhibit the very ftriking figure of Sir *Francis.*

HIS perfon was tall, corpulent, and bony; his face long, pitted with the fmall-pox, without fentiment, and never ornamented with a fmile but to anfwer fome finifter purpofe; and on

this

this occasion it was so very conspicu-
ous, that it may more properly be
termed a convulsion than a simile.
The only tolerable thing about him
had been his hair, which three months
before his tender mother obliged him
to cut off, thinking, perhaps, his head
heavy enough without it : now a round
bob supplied its place, and must have
paid Miss *Coventry* a visit with its mas-
ter, had it not, for that day, been very
fortunately superseded by a magnifi-
cent wig of his father's, whose three
tails dangled on his broad shoulders.
A full-dressed suit of dark green
grogram, richly trimmed with a
broad gold lace, fitted him very nicely
after it was on; though we must
confess, nothing but the most violent
passion for *Maria* could have supported
him in the arduous trial, whilst he
worked, fumed, and tugged to get entrance

trance into the sleeves, &c. His legs
would have been wonderfully hand-
some, if Nature had not, in fixing
them to his body, made a strange mistake, and put that part to his knee,
which must have been designed to
join with his foot. Sir *Francis* had
not himself perceived this mistake, and
thinking them as worthy of notice as
either his head or body, had ornamented them with a pair of crimson
stockings, richly wrought at the ancles,
and gartered very exactly.

WITHOUT exaggeration, such was
the figure of Sir *Francis*: may not
then the inclination for mirth which
his sister betrayed, be esteemed a natural and very excusable emotion?

THE young baronet, on his return
from *Hartly-Row*, found himself as
much

much in love as it was poffible for one
of his difpofition to be, but without
being acquainted with any of the re-
finements of that paffion.

LADY *Gilford* expreffed her approbation of Mifs *Coventry* in high terms;
but neither her Ladyfhip nor her hope-
ful fon were capable of diftinguifhing
that young Lady's value: her lovely
perfon, but more her princely fortune
attracted their notice.

LAVINIA declared Mifs *Coventry* to
be the moft defirable, beautiful, and
accomplifhed woman fhe had ever feen.
" Indeed, brother (faid fhe), you muft
" be extremely happy, if this Lady
" fhould approve your addreffes."

" IF ! (repeated he in a fupercilious
" tone) *if !* Pray, what reafon can
" there

" there be to doubt it? Think you,
" child, Mr. *Coventry* will be fuch a
" fool to refufe a man of my figure?
" a man of fix thoufand a year?—a
" man of title?".

" MR. *Coventry!* (cryed *Lavinia*,
" fmiling) I imagined it was his
" daughter's heart you wanted to fo-
" licit."

" WHY, fhould fhe give it me vo-
" luntary, which I think fhe cannot
" avoid, to confefs the truth, *Levy*, I
" fhould not like my bargain the
" worfe for having it thrown into the
" purchafe."

" I FANCY, Sir, you will find your-
" felf miftaken, if you intend to pur-
" chafe either Mifs *Coventry*'s perfon
" or heart."

" BE

" BE that as it may, I am eafy about
" the matter: however, I fhall have
" one trial with her father. My re-
" liance is on him: he knows, I war-
" rant, how many fhillings make a
" pound."

" FIE, fie, brother!" faid the lovely girl, a blufh of refentment unit-
ing the rofe to the lily; " If thefe
" are your real fentiments, do not re-
" peat them. This afternoon, (con-
" tinued fhe) I wifhed you might mar-
" ry Mifs *Coventry*. That wifh, I own,
" was from a felfifh motive: I was
" ambitious of being related to fuch
" a woman:—I longed to call her
" fifter.—After what you have faid,
" you cannot be deferving fo great a
" treafure."

" AND fie on you, *Lavinia!*" cried
Lady *Gilford*, drawing up her ftiff
neck,

neck, whilft Sir *Francis*'s odious face
was puffed out with paffion; " Fie on
" you, child! Sure you have not con-
" fidered on what you was fo bold, fo
" daring, to fay. Certainly your bro-
" ther is deferving of Mifs *Coventry.*—
" Deferving, indeed! Has he not an
" eftate adequate to her fortune? Has
" he not a title? and a title, girl, is
" not fo lightly to be efteemed."

" OH! you are miftaken, Madam,
" (faid the malicious fnarler, biting
" his blubber lip with vexation)
" you are miftaken; title is a mere
" bawble in her better judgment, or
" fhe would not have refufed my
" friend: fhe would not have carried
" herfelf with fuch haughty airs to Sir
" *William More*, and have taken up
" with a fellow every way his in-
" ferior."

" OH

" OH brother, brother! (replied the
" weeping *Lavinia*) how meanly,
" how cruelly, do you remind me of
" that unhappiness you affifted to
" bring upon me! Do you not blufh
" to call that vile man your friend?——
" He fuperior! Sir *William More* fu-
" perior!——If you have the leaft
" regard to facred truth, inftantly re-
" cal your words, unlefs you meant to
" fay in every kind of wickednefs. If
" that was your meaning, I own, in-
" deed, you are right: greatly in that,
" is Mr. *Gore* inferior to Sir *Wil-*
" *liam!*"

" ROMANTIC girl! (foaming with
" anger) You would, no doubt, run
" after this good-for-nothin g wretch,
" did you but know where to find
" him. No, no, girl, fool as I think
" him, he is too wife for your arts:
" he

" he will not be troubled with you.
" But don't cry, *Levy*, (feeing he had
" brought tears to her eyes) don't cry,
" my pretty forward Mifs; Sir *Wil-*
" *liam* will be here foon, and depend
" on it, you fhall not go without a
" hufband."

" SIR *Francis*, (replied fhe, fpirited
" up by this laft infult) how dare you
" ufe me thus?—What right have
" you to difpofe of me?—I tell you,
" Sir, once again, that all the powers
" on earth fhall never force me to be
" the wife of a man I hate, defpife,
" and loath."

COMPANY coming in at this inftant,
prevented the enraged Sir *Francis* from
making the anfwer he had, no doubt,
meditated, and alfo a fevere reprimand from Lady *Gilford*, who was

ready to ftorm at hearing her darling treated fo freely by his ungracious fifter.

BEFORE the vifitors were feated, *Lavinia* took an opportunity to leave the room, in order to wipe away thofe tears her brother's ill ufage had occa-fioned, and to give a figh to the me-mory of Mr. *Gore*; which being dif-patched, fhe again returned to the drawing-room with a countenance that bore no bad refemblance to an *April* morning. Like that blooming month, her face was dreffed with opening bloffoms: the fnow-drop hung upon her cheek; her eyes were tinged with the violets blue; whilft her breath ex-ceeded the fweetnefs of that flower.

THE company, who all rofe at her entrance, being again replaced, purfued

fued their converfation, which her appearance had interrupted.

Mr. and Mifs *Coventry* were
their topics. The latter, it feems,
was paffing a fevere fcrutiny; and
the two Mifs *Jones*'s had, as they
flattered themfelves, difcovered many
defects in her really faultlefs perfon.
The eldeft with particular energy
pointed them out to Sir *Francis*, who
fhe had long thought a conqueft worth
obtaining.

" I cannot for my life (faid fhe)
" fee thofe thoufand beauties in the
" eyes of Mifs *Coventry*, which my
" coufin *Jack* is continually talking of.
" Only obferve them when you fee her
" next, Sir *Francis*: they are cut fo
" very long!——Well, I proteft their

D 2 " fhape

" fhape do not pleafe me; nor is black
" by any means my favourite co-
" lour."

" INDEED, fifter, (added Mifs *Patty*)
" there is a fweetnefs in them which I
" cannot help thinking agreeable; yet
" I confefs it is very wonderful that a
" young Lady reported to have fo great
" a fhare of fenfe, fhould paint, tho'
" it is laid on very cleverly."

" ODIOUS! (cried Mifs *Jones*) Well,
" that is a fafhion I never could ac-
" commodate myfelf to.—Pray, Sir
" *Francis*, is not her hair two fhades
" lighter than the true chefnut? For
" my part, I have only as yet had a
" tranfient view of this all-excelling
" beauty."

THE

THE Baronet being thus called upon, said, for his part (yawning as he spoke) he was no judge of women's matters: he thought her very well altogether; but rot him if he could tell whether her hair was dark or light.

MR. *Knowles* and Mr. *Nesbit* readily acquiesced with the sentiments of Miss *Jones*, though in their souls each heartily disavowed them; but they were too polite and too well-bred to contradict the Ladies.

MR. *Hunter*, a gentleman not quite so well-bred as the very polite Mr. *Knowles* and Mr. *Nesbit*, having listened patiently, said with a deal of humour, " You are right, Miss *Patty*; " Miss *Coventry* is most certainly " painted:"

By

By Nature alone fhe is painted and dreffed,
Rofes will bloom when there's peace in the
   breaft."

This he fung with fuch an air of re-
proach as made them both blufh,
particularly the perfon to whom he addreffed his fatire.

" Now (continued he) will any
" body allow themfelves to think Mifs
" *Coventry* does not carry peace in her
" breaft ?—How can fhe avoid being
" pleafed and happy, when fhe gains
" a new admirer in every man that
" beholds her ?"

Though, after this reproof, their
envy did not again appear, yet it was
not dead, but only funk back to hearts
in which it had been long nourifhed.

Miss

Miss *Jones's* being lefs perfect mif-
treffes of any other fubject than that
Mr. *Hunter* had interrupted, fpoke
little the remainder of their vifit,
which ended at feven.

If any of my readers after that hour,
in the month of *June*, and the fineft
evening in that month, are inclined
for a folitary walk, I invite them to
attend *Lavinia*, who having tyed on
a ftraw hat lined with blue, and thrown
a handkerchief of the fame colour on
her neck, is proceeding all alone to
that pleafing walk I defcribed in my
firft chapter; her brother ftill too
much irritated to efcort her : rancour
and refentment were weeds which
could not fail to flourifh in a foil fo un-
cultivated, whilft her bofom, forgiv-
ing as Mercy, only fighed at his un-
kindnefs.

D 4 As

As *Lavinia* pursued her walk, she thought incessantly of Mr. *Gore*, and in this manner meditated on her wrongs:

" Alas! (said she) the most worthy
" of men believes me fickle, incon-
" stant;—he shuns,—he flies me;—
" he regards me as the enemy of his
" repose.—Ah! how could they de-
" ceive a heart like his!—Vile, vile Sir
" *William!*——Thy *Machiavelian* arts
" have for ever robbed me of him.—
" Every step I take reminds me of my
" loss.—How applicable to me are
" these beautiful lines I have so often
" read, so often admired, in a sweetly-
" distressing monody:"

" In vain I look around
" O'er all the well-known ground,
" My lover's wonted footsteps to descry!
" Here oft we used to walk,
" Here oft in tender talk
" We saw the summer sun go down the sky."

Lavinia could not suppress her tears at the recollection of past scenes.

" I⊤ is the opinion of a celebrated
" poet, That there is a pleasure in
" madness which none but mad-men
" know ; so it is mine also, that there
" is certainly a pleasure in the enjoy-
" ment of melancholy ideas, which
" none can be a judge of, except those
" to whom they have been familiar."

THOUGH Miss *Gilford*, at this in-
stant, had not a thought but what was
inspired by the goddess *Melpomene*, yet
she would not have exchanged them
to have seen the inimitable *Garrick*, or
to have heard the warblings of a *Pinto*.

THE melody of the latter was well
supplied by a harmonious *Philomel*,

perched

perched on a tree under which *Lavinia* had placed herfelf.

THOSE who underftand the nature of love will alfo know, that paffion is generally attended with fome degree of poetic rapture. *Lavinia* liftened a few moments with fixed attention to the mufical notes of her little feathered companion, and then exclaimed in the words of her moft admired poet :

" With fuch variety and dainty fkill
" Yon nightingale divides her mournful fong,
" As if ten thoufand of them through one bill
" Did fing in parts the ftory of her wrong."

HERE her contemplations were agreeably interrupted by the appearance of Mr. *Coventry* and his fair daughter, who, invited by the ferenity of the evening, were come to this enchanting walk to enjoy it in full perfection.

Lᴀᴠɪɴɪᴀ and *Maria*, who at firſt
fight had been equally prejudiced in
favour of each other, did not try to
hide under the formal maſk of ceremony their mutual pleaſure at this un-
expeͨed meeting.

Lᴀᴠɪɴɪᴀ had high, perhaps romantic notions of friendſhip. The firſt
time ſhe ſaw and converſed with Miſs
Coventry, ſhe thought herſelf convinced, ſhe ſhould in that young Lady
find the phænix ſo many had in vain
ſearched for, a ſincere and tender friend.

Fᴀʀ, very far am I from thinking ſuch a treaſure is never to be attained; neither do I hold it ſo eaſy
an acquiſition as many unexperi-
enced creatures of both ſex believe
it.

WHEN Lord *W——* or Sir *Harry ——* fhakes a thoufand voters by the hand, fwearing to each he is their eternal friend, he proftitutes the name.— Friendfhip is a facred fire. To preferve its flame bright and lafting, it is neceffary to light it up in hearts free from envy, ambition, or any of thefe extinguifhers, as were our firft parents before they had tafted the forbidden fruit, or as the bofoms of *Maria* and *Lavinia.*

TIME was fo agreeably winged with a very pleafing and rational converfation, that they did not obferve the approach of Vefper till fhe had actually wrapped them in her dark mantle.— *Lavinia* was fo much importuned both by Mr. and Mifs *Coventry* to fpend the remainder of this evening (which her company had made fo delightful)

lightful) at *Hartly-Row*, that she at last
confented; and as foon as they reached it, a fervant was difpatched to prevent Lady *Gilford* from being uneafy
at the abfence of her daughter.

SIR *Francis* was with her Ladyfhip
when the meffage came from *Lavinia*,
and in fpite of himfelf could not help
being pleafed at the thoughts of her
cultivating an intimacy with Mr. *Coventry*'s family, into which he hoped
to be very foon received.—Nature having endowed him with a fufficient degree of cunning to enter it on the footing he wifhed, he found it would be
abfolutely neceffary to wear a difguife
till marriage fhould enable him to
throw it off with fafety.

BEING determined to follow his
own ingenious devices, he very wifely
re-

refolved a thorough alteration fhould
be his firft ftep; not an alteration of
heart, but only of manner, regarding
his behaviour to *Lavinia.*

" I am forry, my Lady (faid he)
" that I have taken off the cloaths I
" wore this afternoon; but they were
" fo plaguy tight, I could not fit in
" them with any eafe to myfelf. If I
" had not been in fuch curfed hafte, I
" might have gone to efcort *Levy*
" home from *Hartly-Row*; it would
" have been a d———d good opportu-
" nity."

" And why, my dear (replied her
" Ladyfhip) will you not go as you are?
" You know Mifs *Coventry* has feen
" you full-dreffed. I dare fay fhe does
" not forget the figure you made yef-
" terday afternoon.—Ay, ay, I often
                                    " faw

" faw her eyes fixed on you, *Frank*.
" Come, come, go my dear; I per-
" ceive your mind is fet on it.—She
" muft fome time or other fee you in
" *difhabille*. What fignifies if it be
" this night or a month hence"?

THUS encouraged, he furveyed himfelf from fhoe to wig, turned the latter three or four times on his clumfy
fift, called a fervant, bad him throw
a little powder over it, and bring him
his gold-headed cane, determining at
all events to gratify his inclinations.

ABOUT ten o'clock *Lavinia* was
greatly furprifed to fee him make
his appearance at *Hartly-Row*. That
lowr which ufed to fit on his brow was
intirely banifhed, and good-nature,
though he had only ufurped it for a
time, wrought fuch an alteration, that
he

he paid his respects to Mr. and Miss *Coventry* with a grace that astonished his sister.

" Sir *Francis*, (said that gentle-
" man, shaking him very heartily by
" the hand) as this visit is unexpected,
" we set on it the higher value : but
" let me add, Sir, though I gain one
" pleasure I lose another, as before
" you came I proposed being Miss *Gil-*
" *ford*'s escort to the *Grange*."

" I wish, Sir, (replied Sir *Francis*,
" who was by this time quite a second
" *Cymon*) you had kept your intentions
" a secret: my sister, I fear, will scarce-
" ly pardon me for robbing her of so
" agreeable a conductor; and, upon
" my honour, nothing would make
" me more unhappy than to offend her."

LAVINIA,

LAVINIA, after what had paſſed that day, and indeed for many years, doubted with great reaſon the truth of this aſſertion ; yet ſhe returned him a gracious ſmile, and the higheſt good-humour ſubſiſted till twelve.

NOTWITHSTANDING the ridiculous appearance Sir *Francis* made the pre-ceding day, when his dreſs pronounced him a ſtupid fool and conceited cox-comb, yet, diveſted of theſe enſigns of folly, he was ſo very fortunate as to work a favourable change in the opi-nion of Mr. *Coventry*, who began to regard him as not altogether incapable of rational converſation, and to think the abſurdity of his cloaths rather ow-ing to the narrowneſs of education than from want of underſtanding.

INDEED,

INDEED, he had never fhone half fo
bright as this evening. Luckily no
fubject had been brought on the car-
pet which required any degree of
learning to fupport, and he had the
cunning to adopt fo intirely his fentiments to thofe of the company, that
he appeared to all but *Lavinia* liberal,
compaffionate, humane, in fhort, to
be as full of thofe virtues as he was in
reality of their oppofites ; and he carried on this deceit fo long, till he had
actually impofed it on his fifter.

OFTEN would he beg her pardon
for being the means of preventing her
from marrying Mr. *Gore* ; and one
day he went fo far as to affure her, if
that gentleman fhould ever more return, he would no longer influence his
mother to oppofe their union. "To
" fhew you, *Levy*, that I am fincere
(con-

" (continued he), I am determined to
" break with Sir *William More*. You
" know he expects, on his return from
" *London*, that Lady *Gilford* and I
" shall push the match; but he will
" now find a cold friend in me.—
" In return, may I not expect, *Levy*,
" you will be my advocate with Miss
" *Coventry?*"

" I do promise, brother, to say every
" thing in your favour that can be said
" with justice."

This answer had like to have de-
stroyed his new plan; yet he so well
commanded his passion as not to suffer
it to pass his lips, to prevent which he
bit them most unmercifully.

Recollecting himself for a moment, he replied, " You are very
" oblig-

" obliging, *Levy :*" then saying he was engaged to spend the afternoon with Mr. *Knowles*, he quitted the room, as I shall for some time my pen.

✸✸✸✸✸✸✸✸✸✸✸✸✸✸✸✸✸✸✸✸✸✸✸✸✸✸✸✸✸✸✸✸

CHAP. VIII.

FOUR months had passed since Mr. *Coventry* came to settle at *Weatly*, in which time nothing material happened to our history, except an overture from Sir *Francis* on account of his fair daughter : to which Mr. *Coventry* had replied, that he did him honour ; but having determined in so nice a point not to influence the choice of *Maria*, it must intirely depend on her inclinations either to accept or refuse his offer.

AFTER

AFTER this anfwer, Sir *Francis* feveral times refolved to apply himfelf to the Lady; but notwithftanding the good opinion he had of his own perfon and deferts, whenever he had an opportunity of fpeaking to her, the referve of her manners and the dignity of her appearance awed him into filence.

THOUGH Mifs *Coventry* could not condefcend to any degree of freedom with the brother, to the fifter fhe was without referve, and every day ferved to increafe their friendfhip.

MISS *Coventry* had already told *Lavinia* every thought of her heart. Indeed angels might have known them, they were fo pure, fo like their own. Mifs *Gilford* had not been quite fo explicit; not that hers were lefs innocent,

cent, or needed to be concealed from any other motive than the regard fhe was now beginning to feel for her brother, whofe change of conduct, we muft confefs, was carried on with inimitable management, fince he firft laid down his fcheme of operations.

ONE day Mifs *Coventry* going to the *Grange* to call on *Lavinia,* fhe was told by a fervant his young Lady was gone to walk on the terrace. Not fuffering her to be fent for, fhe tripped through the lawn, where fhe perceived Sir *Francis* and his fifter in deep difcourfe. They did not fee her till fhe came fo near as to hear her own name pronounced by the former; and the furprife they both fhewed at her appearance, confirmed the fufpicion fhe began to entertain that fhe had been

the

the subject of some debate between them.

LONG had she dreaded an explanation of Sir *Francis's* passion; for tho' she gave him many good qualities which in reality he had no pretension to, yet she disliked him with an inconceivable aversion.

LAVINIA had often hinted how happy she should be to call her sister, which she would not have done without believing his disposition intirely altered.

MARIA, who never felt the least tendency to love, either for him or indeed any other person, would on these occasions rally her friend; saying, she estimated liberty so highly, that it was

not

not in the power of an emperor to prevail on her to refign it.

WHEN fhe furprifed them on the
terrace, propofing to take *Lavinia* an
airing, as they had appointed the day
before, it happened that Mifs *Gilford*
had juft then promifed her brother to
feize the next opportunity of a private
moment with her friend to mention
his paffion, which he fwore he never
fhould have courage to do himfelf.

SIR *Francis* having handed the Ladies to their chariot with the grimace
of politenefs (for with real politenefs
he was intirely unacquainted) gave his
fifter's hand a gentle fqueeze to remind
her of her promife ; and intending to
fee Mifs *Coventry* either at the *Grange*
or *Hartly-Row* after her return, he
was going to prepare his fweet perfon
for

for the interview; not in the antique cloaths of his father, but a modern fuit of pompadour and filver juft imported from *London*, with a wig, fword, hat, &c. of the neweft mode.

BEFORE he begun to drefs, the arrival of Sir *William More* difconcerted his intentions; and notwithftanding all he had promifed his fifter, he gave the baronet a reception very far from cold or difcouraging : and as the company of his friend would prevent him from a vifit that evening to his miftrefs, he determined to confole himfelf by a free enjoyment of his bottle; a liberty he had for fome time retrenched, with his other ill qualities.

WE fha'l leave this brace of worthies at a table with excellent claret before them, and go back to the Ladies.

LA-

LAVINIA had not forgot her engagement to Sir *Francis*, but found Mifs *Coventry* fo very determined not to receive his addreffes, that fhe refolved never more to mention fo unpleafing a fubject.

THOUGH Mifs *Gilford* in reality did not look the leaft grave, yet the regard *Maria* had for her made that young Lady fancy fhe faw a cloud on her countenance; and taking her hand with the moft engaging franknefs, " Do " not, my dear Mifs *Gilford*, (faid fhe) " make me unhappy in withdrawing " your friendfhip. If I refufe your " brother, it is from the fame motive " I fhould do the addreffes of all the " men I have ever yet feen. Perhaps " my fentiments of love may be too " refined. How many do we every " day fee marry with indifference, yet " live

" live what the world calls tolerably
" happy!—Poſſibly they may; but I
" will never make the trial : I have no
" idea of what is meant by tolerable
" happineſs.—Do you think, *Lavinia*,
" my notions of that ſtate are too high,
" when I tell you that to me it appears
" a faint reſemblance of what we are
" to expeÿt in another world, either
" extreme felicity, or unceaſing tor-
" ment ?"

" THESE ſentiments (replied Miſs
" *Gilford*) I expeÿted from you. My
" brother muſt reſign himſelf to his
" fate ; ſuch a heart as yours he never
" can merit ; yet I will love you as a
" ſiſter, though you refuſe to give me a
" title to the name."

NOTHING could be more agreeable
than this declaration to the perſon for

whom

whom it was intended.—She returned
the moſt ſincere profeſſions of eſteem,
and they continued their little excur-
ſion, delighted in the company of each
other.

" My dear, (ſaid *Lavinia*, as they
" purſued the great road) about two
" miles from this, place is one of Na--
" ture's rude beauties, but ſo ſweetly
" pleaſing, that if you are inclined for
" contemplation, I will convey you to
" it, and you ſhall confeſs no ſpot was
" ever better calculated to inſpire either
" the moſt gloomy or the moſt chear-
" ful ideas."

" You have raiſed my curioſity to
" ſo high a pitch (ſaid Miſs *Coventry*),
" that poſitively you muſt give me a
" deſcription of this wonderful place
" before we reach it."

" NOT

" NOT a word of defcription," replied *Lavinia*; and pulling the ftring
ordered the coachman to drive immediately to *Combe-Woods*.

AGAIN Mifs *Coventry* renewed her
intreaties, but to no purpofe; *Lavinia*
continued obftinately filent to all her
inquiries.—Striking out of the beaten
road, and entering one almoft impaf-
fible, they continued dragging through
narrow lanes till all of a fudden, at
the end of one of them, the carriage
ftopped, a fervant opened the door,
and Mifs *Gilford* ftepping out defired
her friend to follow.

" FOLLOW (faid Mifs *Coventry*)!
" Where the duce, my dear, would
" you lead (at the fame time getting
" out)? If you mean to fhew me
" any remarkable view, I am fure we
E 3   " muft

" muſt climb one of theſe high elms
" to command it."

" TRUST yourſelf to my conduct
" (replied *Lavinia*), and you ſhall nei-
" ther climb or creep to attain the
" promiſed land." Then taking hold
of her arm, ſhe turned ſhort upon
the right ; and all at once ſtartled *Maria* by introducing her to a ſmall but
beautiful common, ſurrounded by natural woods, and above them hills of a
thouſand variegated colours, on the
ſides of which ſhe pointed out both the
Grange and *Hartly-Row*, with many
other pretty looking houſes.

OBSERVING how much *Maria* was
delighted with this little ſpot, ſhe ſaid
to her, " Here it is, Miſs *Coventry*,
" if you would indulge chearful ideas,
" you may do it freely. If you are
                              " more

" more inclined to the gloomy, I
" will lead you to another retreat."

" I AM fo pleafed, fo tranfported,
" (returned *Maria*) with this fweet en-
" chanting place, that I fhould be loth
" to leave it, if I had not a ftrong in-
" clination to have my whole curiofity
" fatisfied; fo lead on, I befeech you,
" to the gloomy: not that I have any
" thoughts to indulge there, I'll affure
" you."

LAVINIA fighed.———" This place
" (faid fhe) is called *Combe-Woods*, and
" thought fo very curious, that it is of-
" ten vifited by ftrangers; otherwife
" it would be perfectly unfrequented,
" none of the neighbourhood ever
" coming hither; the common peo-
" ple having entertained a ftrange no-
" tion, that it is the habitation of fu-

E 4   " per-

" pernatural beings; and thofe of fupe-
" rior rank having fatisfied their curio-
" fity feldom take the trouble of com-
" ing again."

By this time they were entered the
furrounding woods.

" AH ! (faid Mifs *Coventry*) this, in-
" deed, may be called a fit place for
" melancholy reflections. Here, (con-
" tinued fhe, feating herfelf on an old
" tree felled by the hand of Time)
" let us on this friendly trunk enjoy
" them.　But having none of my
" own, *Lavinia*, I charge you let me
" partake of yours.——Yes, my dear,
" it is in vain to deny it; you have fe-
" crets; painful ones too, or I am
" miftaken.　I have heard you figh
" often.——Certainly you do not figh
" without a caufe.

" HEIGH-

" HEIGH-ho!"

" THERE it is again.—Declare im-
" mediately the happy fwain who—"

SHE was proceeding, when Mifs *Gil-*
ford interrupted her: " Cannot you in-
" fpire me with fome fmall fhare of
" your charming vivacity?"—

" NOT a tittle (fhe returned), till
" you lighten that heart of yours, by
" giving me the huge fecret it carries.
" —Do this, and I will engage to
" make you as blithe as a lark."

" WHAT you promife, is not in your
" power to perform (faid *Lavinia*); I
" can never more be chearful! I can
" never again be happy!"

" HEAVENS! How you furprife,
" how you terrify me! If you had
" troubles, why did you not make me
E 5 " a fharer

" a fharer in them ?—Indeed it was
" unkind !—Indeed I fhould not have
" treated you with fo little confidence!"

" PARDON me, *Maria,* I had rea-
" fon till now for concealment. My
" brother muft have fuffered in your
" opinion: his hopes are now at an
" end, and you fhall no longer tax
" me with referve."

" THANK you, my dear *Lavinia;*
" we have yet an hour good before
" we need leave this charming place.
" You have alarmed my fears for you;
" in pity, then, make hafte to relieve
" them. If you are unhappy, it is the
" office of friendfhip to take a fhare
" in your concern."

Miss *Gilford* faw the impatience of
Maria, and addreffed her as may be
found in the next chapter.

CHAP.

CHAP. IX.

" ABOUT two years since I was
" unfortunate enough to be ap-
" proved of by Sir *William More*; a
" man——"

" NAY, my dear, (interrupted Mifs
" *Coventry*) fpare yourfelf the trouble
" of giving me his character: I have
" already received it from my father.
" Surely your friends could not en-
" courage a wretch of fuch abandoned
" morals!"

" I KNOW not what to fay in their
" vindication (replied *Lavinia*); riches
" often fafcinate the fenfes, making

E 6.   " people

" people and things appear quite dif-
" ferent from what they really are.
" Light faults in perfons of narrow
" fortune are aggravated to a furprifing
" magnitude ; whilft an opulent man
" may be guilty of the greateft enor-
" mities, and pafs them on the partial
" world for lively fallies, frolicks, and
" many other much too gentle appel-
" lations.   A king can do no wrong,
" is a faying I have often heard ; nor,
" in fome people's opinion, can men
" on whom Fortune has beftowed her
" favours.   This I found to be the
" cafe in refpect to Sir *William More*.
" When I objected to his love of drink,
" All men that were not milk-fops
" would fometimes take a chearful
" glafs :"——his libertine principles,
" Thefe were affertions of his ene-
" mies :"——his being addicted to fwear-
" ing, fcarce a word being unattended
                                " by

" by a horrid oath, " No sign of a bad
" heart; only a foolish habit, and
" easily conquered."

" GOOD heavens! (exclaimed *Ma-*
" *ria*) sure Lady *Gilford* could never
" argue thus."

" No, no; this conversation passed
" with my brother, who had ever been
" the sworn friend of Sir *William.*
"———I see resentment rising in your
" bosom, Madam (continued she); I
" know you do, I know you must
" blame me for attempting to preju-
" dice you in favour of Sir *Francis*;
" but had I not thought his very dif-
" ferent from the principles of Sir
" *William More*; had I not thought
" he now utterly despised that wretch;
" had I not believed him the most al-
" tered man in the world; that he loved
" my

" my dear Mifs *Coventry* with the moſt
" ſincere and fervent paſſion, and that
" he would ſuffer in his health by
" concealing it longer; I ſhould never
" have mentioned a ſubject which I
" determined to drop, as ſoon as I ſaw
" it was diſpleaſing."

MISS *Coventry* had no longer any
cloud on her countenance; ſhe grace-
fully aſſured *Lavinia* of her entire
friendſhip, and with a ſweet ſmile
begged ſhe would proceed in a recital
that had already filled her with impatience.

" EIGHTEEN months have I been
" teized, my dear Mifs *Coventry*, with
" the addreſſes of Sir *William More* ;
" my brother, and conſequently my
" mother, till now ſtrenuous in his fa-
" vour; notwithſtanding which I al-
                   " ways

" ways declared myfelf very freely,
" that I never would be his.

" ABOUT ten months fince, being
" much preffed by the advocates of Sir
" *William* to attend them at a ball he
" gave, and finding it impoffible to
" get myfelf excufed, I very reluctantly
" complied.—We entered the room,
" happily for me, before Sir *William* ;
" who finding me engaged at his arri-
" val, curfed the bufinefs that had de-
" tained him, and would not dance
" the whole evening, but fat in a cor-
" ner by himfelf, fullen and out of hu-
" mour, except when he could engage
" me in converfation, which I took
" care fhould be very feldom.

" I AM not going to defcribe the
" gentleman with whom I danced, as
" I know myfelf incapable of doing
" him

" him juftice; I fhall only fay, his
" converfation had in it fomething fo
" elegantly refined, as that very even-
" ing got him a footing in my efteem,

" Notwithstanding the com-
" pany did not part till three, I never
" thought any time fo fhort.

" On our way home, I'afked my
" brother if he knew the gentleman
" who had been my parties.

" He faid his name was *Gore*, and
" on a vifit to Mr. *Willace*.

" He has loft fome near relation, I
" fuppofe (replied I), by his being in
" fuch clofe mourning.

" His father (he returned) is lately
" dead, and has left him an eftate of
                        " two

" two thoufand pounds a year; but
" methinks, *Levy*, you are very inqui-
" fitive : I hope you do not mean to let
" him fupplant Sir *William*."

" SUPPLANT Sir *William!* (repeated
" I); furely, brother, you might have
" fpared the fuppofition. What is Sir
" *William More* to me? How often
" fhall I repeat to you, that I never
" will think of him in the light you
" propofe him."

" PERVERSE girl!" faid my mother.

" My brother did not confine him-
" felf, on this occafion, even to com-
" mon decency; he fwore I fhould
" marry his friend.

" INDEED, child, you muft (added
" her Ladyfhip); you muft, and fhall
" be Lady *More*."

" NEVER, never, Madam! whilſt
" I exiſt, I will never be Sir *William*'s !"

" THE coach ſtopping prevented a
" very angry anſwer; and as ſoon as
" the door was opened, I ſtepped out,
" and flew to my apartment, where
" I ſpent the remainder of the night in
" a manner not to be envied.

" I NEVER cloſed my eyes to ſleep
" till ſeven; and when *Sally* came to
" call me at ten, I was enjoying that
" refreſhing inſenſibility.

" HAVING awakened me by un-
" drawing my curtains, I aſked if
" breakfaſt was ready. She told me
" no; but added, " I have a letter for
" you, Madam."

" I ſtarted up in my bed, I broke
" the ſeal with eagerneſs, and found it

" contained two cards; one from Mr.
" *Gore*, addreſſed to me, with polite
" inquiries after my health; the other
" to my mother, from Mrs. *Willace*, to
" ſay they would be with us in the af-
" ternoon, if her Ladyſhip was diſen-
" gaged.

" I GOT up immediately, and went
" to my mother's room, which ſhe
" had juſt left, and I found her in the
" breakfaſt-parlour with Sir *Francis*.

" I GAVE the card intended for her
" Ladyſhip, but ſaid not a word of
" mine, for fear of renewing their
" ſuſpicions.

" AFTER having glanced it over,
" ſhe put it into the hands of my bro-
" ther, who returned it with his opi-
" nion, that they could not avoid ſee-
" ing

" ing them, as Sir *William* and other
" company were expected.

" In fhort, Madam, Mr. *Gore* came
" with them ; that vifit was productive
" of a fecond ;—that fecond of a third ;
" and every time I faw him I was
" more and more convinced of his re-
" gard for me : we felt the warmeft
" fentiments of friendfhip for each
" other, and did not attempt to con-
" ceal them."

" How prettily, my dear, (faid *Ma-*
" *ria,* interrupting her) you fubftitute
" the word Friendfhip to fupply that
" of Love: but you are certainly right ;
" the latter fhould always be founded
" on the former. Love is a mift which
" feldom continues longer than the
" morning of life. If friendfhip,
" like the fun, appears warm and
                                " bright

" bright to fucceed it, we are affured of
" a fine day : if the contrary, ftorms,
" clouds, and tempeft, are to be ex-
" pected."

" CHARMINGLY imagined! (repli-
" ed *Lavinia*.) Indeed, to confefs the
" truth, my friendfhip for Mr. *Gore*
" might have bore another appellation,
" if I had not, like my dear Mifs *Co-*
" *ventry*, taken the terms of love and
" friendfhip to be almoft fynonymous.

" HOWEVER, give it which name
" you pleafe, the fentiment we mu-
" tually felt, was as mutually acknow-
" ledged ; and nothing but my mo-
" ther's confent feemed wanting to
" complete our happinefs.

" I HAD the pleafure to think Mr.
" *Gore* enjoyed a confiderable fhare in
" her

" her efteem.—How, indeed, could
" he avoid it? Were not her eyes, her
" ears formed of the fame materials
" as thofe of her unhappy daughter?

" At laft he laid open his inten-
" tions, and was liftened to with fome
" degree of condefcenfion, his offers
" of fettlement being extremely no-
" ble: however, fhe told him, before
" he could expect a definitive anfwer,
" fhe muft confult her fon; and if he
" would give up the intereft of Sir
" *William More*, fhe fhould then have
" no objection to his alliance.

" But on confulting my brother,
" and finding him more ftrenuous than
" ever for his friend, her behaviour to
" Mr. *Gore* underwent an immediate
" change; and without the leaft apo-
" logy, fhe defired him to defift from
" his

" his vifits, as Sir *Francis* had engaged
" his promife to Sir *William More*, and
" would by no means break it.

" HE begged, he prayed, he in-
" treated, he expoftulated; but in vain.
" —Would my mother, he afked,
" oblige me to marry a man to whom
" I had fo often declared my averfion?
" —He was anfwered, That intermed-
" dlers were not looked on by her in
" an advantageous light :—That they
" had great reliance on my duty, if he
" did not attempt to fet it afide.

" STRUCK to the foul by this reply,
" he had fcarce command enough over
" himfelf to confider it was my mo-
" ther who treated him with fo much
" difrepect: however, no fooner had
" he made this reflection, than he left
" the houfe, only faying, as his vifits
" were

" were fo very difagreeable, he would
" endeavour not to repeat them.

" On my return from Mifs *Leafon's*,
" where I had fpent the afternoon, I
" was furprifed not to find Mr. *Gore*
" at the *Grange*, having appointed to
" pafs the evening with us : but what
" did I feel, when told by my unkind
" mother, and I muft fay cruel bro-
" ther, that if ever I expeded to be
" looked on as the child of the one,
" as the fifter of the other, I muft ab-
" folutely promife never to fee Mr.
" *Gore*, or at leaft fpeak to him again,
" and inftantly determine to accept
" the hand of Sir *William*.

" The moft explicit duty furely
" could not have demanded a facri-
" fice like this : I refufed to make it,
" and their anger was raifed to fuch a
" height,

" that I was forced to fly to my cham-
" ber to avoid its fevere effects.

" A LETTER from Mr. *Gore*, which
" *Sally* conveyed to me, ferved to
" heighten the load of grief I felt.—
" How kind, how tender, how ge-
" neroufly did he intreat that I would
" become the abfolute miftrefs of his
" fortune, as I already was of his
" heart!—His very exiftence, he faid,
" depended on the refolution I had
" made, never to have Sir *William*.

" My anfwer was dictated by a fin-
" cere regard; and another letter,
" which I foon received, convinced me
" it was far from difpleafing him.

" A RÉGULAR correfpondence was
" now fettled between us, *Sally* being
" our agent; for though Mr. *Gore*

" ſtill continued with his friend Mr.
" *Willace*, I was too cloſely watched
" even for a ſingle interview : and had
" it not been for the pleaſure his let-
" ters afforded me, I muſt in this ſitu-
" ation have found myſelf extremely
" miſerable, being reduced to the diſ-
" agreeable neceſſity of hearing pro-
" feſſions of love from the wretch I
" moſt on earth deſpiſed.

" Sir *William* was almoſt become
" an inmate in our family, and my
" brother fearing my averſion would
" at length tire out his paſſion, deter-
" mined with my mother's acquieſ-
" cence to oblige me to marry him, in
" ſpight of objections.

" They firſt tried to gain their ends
" by affectionate intreaties. If any
" method could have prevailed, it muſt
" have

" have been this : the large settlement
" and blaze of jewels, that next made
" an appearance on the persuasive list,
" were equally ineffectual.

" THIS obstinacy, as my steady re-
" fusal was called, provoked Sir *Fran-*
" *cis* to such a height, that he swore I
" should marry his friend before the
" next *Thursday*, or he would not live
" in *England* another week.

" My mother, terrified by this
" threat, and seeing him leave the
" room in a rage, loaded me with re-
" proaches which it pains me to recol-
" lect.

" I FELL on my knees, and with
" tears intreated she would not sacri-
" fice me to my brother's cruel ca-
" price; that she would not give her

sanction

" fanction to my being made the moft
" miferable of wretches.

" Very pretty, very pretty, Ma-
" dam! replied my mother: I per-
" ceive whence all this proceeds; but
" if you will not have Sir *William*, you
" fhall not have *Gore*; depend on that."

" No, Madam, (faid I, rifing from
" my fupplicating pofture) no, it is not
" the idea of Mr. *Gore* that obftructs
" my union with Sir *William:* before
" I knew the one, I abhorred the
" other. Reflect impartially but for
" a moment : Can the knowledge of
" fo much worth as Mr. *Gore* poffeffes,
" leffen my averfion to his detefted
" rival ?"

" Fie, fie, girl! Detefted ! Is that
" a proper word for the man who
                               " muft,

" muſt, who ſhall, I am determined
" ſhall be your huſband ?"

" THE hated Sir *William* coming in
" at this inſtant, deaf to his ſolicita-
" tions, and almoſt to the commands
" of my mother, I retired to my
" chamber."

CHAP.

CHAP. X.

" HAVING compofed my fpirits,
" I wrote to Mr. *Gore* what had
" paffed; at the fame time bidding
" him depend on my refolution never
" to take a ftep which would give him
" reafon to upbraid me.

" Mr. *Willace's* was not more than
" a mile from the *Grange*, and *Sally*
" returned in lefs than an hour :—but,
" O my God! with what an account
" of Mr. *Gore's* frenzy! Indeed the
" few diftracted lines he fent would
" have fpoke it, had fhe been filent."

" CAN

" CAN you remember (afked Mifs
" *Coventry*) what they were?"

" PERFECTLY (replied *Lavinia*)."

" TALK to me not (faid he) of next
" *Thurfday!*—Talk to me not of your
" refolution! What, my gentle *Lavi-*
" *nia,* will avail your refiftance?—
" Perhaps the deed on which I am re-
" folved, may be wrong!—I will not,
" cannot drop it. Blame me not, my
" love! I muft not lofe you!—Angels
" protect and guard my deareft *La-*
" *vinia!*"

MARIA, who was kindly wiping
the tears from Mifs *Gilford's* cheek,
foon found by the trickling drop that
glided down her own, that fhe had
caught the foft infection.

" How

" How my heart (faid fhe) bleeds
" for my diftreffed *Lavinia!* But my
" impatience will not fuffer me to fay
" with what tender fympathy. Hea-
" vens! proceed, pray proceed! I am
" all fear, all dread! Mr. *Gore* is cer-
" tainly killed by the detefted Sir *Wil-*
" *liam.*"

" No, my dear Mifs *Coventry*, I am
" not fo very, very unhappy as that
" would have made me: he ftill lives,
" though for ever dead, for ever loft
" to me."

" THANK God, he lives! (cried
" her friend) he cannot, fhall not be
" loft to you! But tell me why you
" accufe him of infidelity?"

" FAR be it from me to accufe him
" of infidelity, replied *Lavinia:* hear
" the

" the fequel of my ftory, and be your-
" felf the judge.

" No fooner had I read his letter,
" than I was rendered infenfible by the
" violent fhock it gave me. *Sally* did
" not call any one to my afliftance, but
" laid me on the bed, and with her
" endeavours to bring me to my fenfes,
" I began to recover enough to know
" what it was that occafioned my in-
" fenfibility.

" It immediately occurred to me
" that Sir *William* might be ftill with
" my mother ; and not knowing what
" I did, or paying the leaft attention
" to *Sally*'s remonftrances, I haftened
" down ftairs, my drefs in the greateft
" diforder, and burfting open the door
" I entered the room with fuch a wild-
" nefs in my air and manner, as quite

F 5   " terrified

" terrified my mother: but not feeing
" the perfon there whom I came in
" purfuit of, my fears redoubled, and
" I exclaimed in words fcarce articu-
" late,

" Where, O my God! where is
" Sir *William*?

" Her Ladyfhip had the goodnefs,
" feeing me fo agitated, to take my hand,
" and feating me by her, enquired into
" the caufe of my perturbations; but
" inftead of anfwering her queftion,
" I repeated my own, Where, where
" is Sir *William*?—How long has
" he left you? Was he fent for?"

" Yes, (faid my mother) he was
" fent for to a gentleman on particular
" bufinefs."

" Then

" THEN all is over! all is over,
" Madam! Yet hafte to fave the life
" of the man you favour; and O fave,
" if poffible, the life of him for whom
" I would gladly refign my own!"

" EXPLAIN, *Lavinia*, or how will
" it be poffible to do either?"

" HAVING given the beft account
" my fluttered fpirits would allow, fhe
" left the room with a precipitation
" equal to my wifhes.

" AFTER her Ladyfhip had dif-
" patched half a dozen fervants to
" prevent the fate of her intended fon-
" in-law, fhe came back, doubtlefs
" with a defign to read me a lecture
" on the dreadful effects of difobedi-
" ence, and to reprimand me for car-
" rying on a private correfpondence
F 6 " with

" with Mr. *Gore*, but found a fitter
" object for compaffion than feverity.

" A second time I was extended
" on the floor, from which being re-
" moved to my bed, I lay a fortnight
" without the leaft hope of reco-
" very. So violent a fever fucceeded
" my fainting, that I did not fpeak
" during that time; yet I remember
" my mother was very affiduous about
" me, and more than once I faw her
" fhed tears.

" One day, as fhe was fitting by
" my bed-fide, I took her hand, and
" faintly pronounced the name of
" Mr. *Gore*.

" I know, *Levy*, (replied her Lady-
" fhip) what you would fay, and give
" you my honour that Mr. *Gore* is fafe."

" I lifted

"I LIFTED up my hands and eyes,
" in gratitude to heaven for this in-
" telligence.

"I NOW every day gathered ftrength,
" I wanted much an opportunity of
" fpeaking to *Sally* ; but fhe appeared
" as ftudious to avoid, as I did to pro-
" cure it.

"HER Ladyfhip being called to a
" perfon on bufinefs, I faid to her,
" Come hither, *Sally* ; why have you
" not before this contrived fome means
" to tell me how Mr. *Gore* came off
" in the duel he had with Sir *William?*

"DUEL! replied fhe ; a duel,
" Madam! I know of none. Thefe
" gentlemen have never fought."

"THANK

"THANK God! faid I; then I
"may ftill be happy. I am fure no-
"thing lefs than Sir *William*'s refign-
"ing his pretenfions could have pre-
"vented the event I dreaded."

"I FANCY it is not fo neither, Ma-
"dam; for Sir *William* is here every
"day to enquire after your health: it
"was not five minutes fince I faw him
"below."

"You furprife me, *Sally!*—Not
"fight!—Sir *William* come ftill to the
"houfe!——Have you received no
"letters for me?"

"I HAVE had one, Madam, more
"than a week, but could not find an
"opportunity to deliver it till now."—

"MY

" My mother coming in at that in-
" ſtant, made me hide it in the bed,
" till I could find a proper time to read
" it, which, alas ! came but too ſoon.

" The ſurpriſe, the aſtoniſhment,
" the grief I felt was inexpreſſible,
" when, inſtead of telling me what
" he ſuffered from my illneſs, to be
" told, and in the moſt aggravating
" terms, that I was no longer worthy
" his regard ; that he had once thought
" my heart the throne of conſtancy,
" but found it was only an appearance
" of that virtue.—He bid me ſtill be
" happy, though it was not now in
" my power, nor in that of any other
" woman, to make him ſo."

" Oh the horrid ingrate ! exclaim-
" ed Miſs *Coventry* ; how I hate, how
" I deteſt him !"

       " Let

" Let not appearances deceive you;
" (replied *Lavinia*) I cannot bear that
" he fhould lie under your difpleafure
" even for a moment. I am impa-
" tient to clear him ; but we muft talk
" on this fubject in the carriage : we
" do not feem to confider it is fix miles
" to *Weatly*, and that the fun has al-
" moft kiffed the fea."

Maria, who could have fat till
midnight without counting hours whilft
fhe liftened to *Lavinia*, thus reminded, arofe from her humble feat, when
a ruftling of the boughs made them
turn round, and they ftarted at feeing
a man within a few yards of them.

The mild fweetnefs that fhone upon
his face forbade fear. Some thoufand
years before, he might have been miftaken for the Genius of the woods.—
The

THE filver beard which hung half way down his waiſt caught their attention, and *Lavinia* whiſpered *Maria* to obſerve his graceful movement, as he came towards them.

WHEN he ſpoke, they felt a veneration for him they could by no means account for.

" You are doubtlefs furprifed, my
" daughters, (faid he) at the fight of a
" man of fuch uncommon appearance.
" Believe me, (turning to Mifs *Gil-*
" *ford*) I came not to this place to be
" a liftener: No ; I came to contem-
" plate my own misfortunes, and weep
" afrefh at their remembrance : but
" you have robbed them of their daily
" tribute ; your ſtory has ſtole from me
" thoſe tears which were due to them."

" I AM

" I am forry, Sir, (fhe replied) tho'
" inadvertently, that I fhould have in
" the leaft diftreffed you; finding too,
" by your words, you are not on your
" own account exempt from trouble."

"Indeed I am not (returned the
" pious ftranger); but though I have
" had a double portion of afflictions,
" I blefs God continually, and doubt
" not the wifdom of his defign in fend-
" ing them.——Pardon me, Ladies, I
" had a requeft to make; particularly,
" Madam, I muft addrefs myfelf to
" you," added he, fpeaking to Mifs
Gilford.

" It is already granted, Sir," fhe
replied with a moft enchanting grace.

" You know not, my good young
" Lady, the extent of my boldnefs;
" yet

" yet term it not idle curiofity, when
" I tell you I wifh much to hear the
" fequel of that relation you have
" been juft giving your friend, and to
" which I liftened not from a bad
" motive.—You fay (continued he) you
" can clear the feeming infidelity of
" your lover."

" INDEED, Sir, I can ; and if you
" will meet us here to-morrow after-
" noon, I will give you the fequel
" you defire."

" EXCELLENT goodnefs ! he re-
" turned : I pray Heaven all your
" diftreffes may foon have an end, and
" that you may again meet and be
" united to the perfon who has the
" happinefs to be efteemed by you !—
" And may this other flower, this fif-
" ter-fweetnefs, (turning to Mifs *Co-*
" *ventry*,

" *ventry*, taking a hand of each) make
" happy fome man deferving fo much
" innocence, fo much beauty! O my
" God! fuch a one you once lent me!"

" AH, my good Sir! (faid *Maria*)
" you afflict us greatly. See Mifs *Gil-*
" *ford's* eyes; look at mine; they
" overflow to think a man fo worthy
" as you feem to be, fhould labour
" under the oppreffion of forrow. Do
" not deny me a boon I am about to
" afk; if you fhould, it would almoft
" break my heart."

" SPEAK, my child (faid the vene-
" rable ftranger); if within my power
" to oblige you, fuch fweetnefs fhall
" not afk in vain."

" I AM going, Sir, (replied fhe with
" an enchanting fmile) to be very in-
                              " quifitive.

" quifitive. In the firft place, will you
" condefcend to inform us to what na-
" tion you belong ? for I imagine you
" are not a native of this kingdom."

He fmiled at her furmife.—" I have
" never (returned he) feen any other
" kingdom; but I can eafily account,
" Madam, for your miftake. My
" uncommon habit, and this length
" of hair (pointing to his chin) muft
" make me appear extremely ftrange
" to people who are converfant with
" the world: but as I am not obliged
" to ftudy its fafhions, my only care is
" to provide the abfolute neceffaries of
" life. You will fcarce credit me (con-
" tinued he) when I tell you, that, ex-
" cept yourfelves and three other per-
" fons, I have not feen a human face
" thefe five years."

" Where,

" Where, said *Lavinia*; Where,
" said *Maria*; can you have been all
" this time fequeftered ?"

" Before I difcover that, (he re-
" plied) you muft give me a folemn
" promife never to difclofe it without
" my permiffion. On thefe condi-
" tions, to-morrow, when you return,
" I will lead you to my retreat."

" We fubfcribe to them with plea-
" fure," faid they : " Though (added
" Mifs *Coventry*) I now perceive the
" boon I intended to afk muft be given
" up. I was going (purfued fhe) to
" petition you would go with us to my
" father's. He is a good man ; he re-
" veres good men : how would he be
" delighted with your company ! If you
" fhould then weep, his tears would
" fall with yours : he has loft a wife,

" I a

" I a mother, for whom they will ever
" flow."

" YOUR father has loſt a wife, you
" ſay, my good young Lady: I too
" have loſt one, the pattern of every
" virtue, every excellence. Perhaps ſo
" was his; but has he loſt children,
" friends, fortune, all that in this life
" is deſirable? O no! he has not;
" you are his daughter. What a bleſ-
" ſing, what a treaſure has he ſtill
" left! How unfit for companions!
" Whenever we ſat down to enumerate
" our misfortnnes, his tale of woe
" would ſoon be told, whilſt mine
" would laſt from morn to eve, from
" eve to morn, a ſummer's day."

THE compaſſionate tear quivered
in the bright eyes of *Lavinia* and *Ma-*
ria: they longed to know what thoſe
                                    miſ-

misfortunes were, and why he had banifhed himfelf from mankind; but were forced to fufpend their curiofity, as the night made fuch fwift approaches.

AFTER renewing their promife of fecrecy, alfo of meeting early the following day, they parted; the Ladies regained their carriage, whilft the ftranger ftruck into the thickeft part of the woods.

IT is impoffible to fay how much they wifhed for the next afternoon: they thought nor talked of any thing but their late adventure, till arrived within a mile of *Weatly*, when it was banifhed the breaft of *Lavinia* by the fight of Sir *William More*, feated in his Phaeton, but indebted to a fervant from undergoing the fame fate with

that

that prefumptuous youth whofe name his carriage bore; the Baronet's head being nearly as giddy with claret, as the offspring of *Apollo* was with ambition.

Passing the chariot where fat his miftrefs, he attempted to fpeak; but it was only an attempt.

" Heavens! (faid Mifs *Coventry*) " what a beaft is that which has juft " paffed us! Lord help me! Why, my " dear Mifs *Gilford*, do you change " colour?"

" Ah Madam! (replied *Lavinia*) " that is the detefted Sir *William*, re- " turned to make me miferable. All " my reliance now is on Sir *Francis*, " who has affured me he will no more " intereft himfelf in his favour."

" Well

" WELL then, my dear, why are " you apprehenfive ?"

" I CERTAINLY ought not to alarm " myfelf (returned Mifs *Gilford*) ; but " in his very appearance there is a " fomething to me ftrangely terrify- " ing."

THE remainder of their journey fhe feemed fo much fluttered, and fo very uneafy, that Mifs *Coventry*, who thought it poffible fhe might meet Sir *William* if fhe returned to the *Grange*, obliged her to pafs the night at *Hartly-Row*, after fending an excufe to Lady *Gilford* by the fervant who attended them, informing her Ladyfhip *Lavinia* would fpend the next day with Mifs *Coventry*.

WHEN

WHEN the chariot ſtopped at the door, doctor *Edgcome* preſented his hand, and helped the Ladies to alight.

I OUGHT to aſk my readers pardon for not introducing this worthy gentle-man to them ſince the death of Mrs. *Co-ventry*, eſpecially as he had been a great aſſiſtant to his patron in forming the mind of his amiable daughter. The love he bore that young Lady was little in-ferior to what might be felt by a pa-rent: this he ſhewed in refuſing a va-luable living, which, had he accepted, muſt have divided him from the deareſt of his friends.

DOCTOR *Edgcome*'s converſation ſoftened many uneaſy reflections in the breaſt of Mr. *Coventry*, his diſpoſition being extremely chearful; which

chear-

chearfulneſs he derived from an approving heart. His glaſs had few remaining ſands to run: already he attained an honourable old age, yet hitherto ſuch a favourite of Providence, that he had not groaned under any of its pains and inconveniences.

C H A P.

CHAP. XI.

MR. *Coventry*, as his daughter did not return till the clock had ſtruck nine, began to be alarmed, fearing ſome accident; but when ſhe entered the room, and flew into his parental arms, expanded to receive her, every uneaſy ſenſation vaniſhed.

" Is this the way (ſaid doctor *Edg-*
" *come*, ſmiling) that you puniſh our
" runaway? Your daughter would be
" ſpoiled, was it not for me."

" INDEED, Sir, (cried *Maria*) you
" really frightened me; but I ſhould
G 3
" have

" have known, if my dear Papa had
" been difpleafed with his girl, you
" would not have told me fo with that
" ferenity of countenance."

" Love you! (interrupted the face-
" tious old gentleman) Really, my
" friend, (turning to Mr. *Coventry*) I
" was in hopes we might have paffed
" fome years longer together; but that
" will be now impoffible; for after a
" young fellow like me is difcovered
" to be a lover, the world will talk,
" whilft he continues in the fame houfe
" with the object of his paffion."

" Upon my honour, (faid Mr. *Co-*
" *ventry*) as you ftate the matter, Doc-
" tor, I know not how to advife. Mifs
" *Gilford*, what is your opinion?"

" Why,

"Why really, Sir, fince I muft
"fpeak, though I fhould be forry to
"fill you with fufpicions, I believe if
"the doctor leaves you, there is fome
"danger of *Lavinia*'s eloping with
"him; for by what I have obferved,
"their paffion feems to be mutual."

"Miss *Gilford* fays true, Sir (re-
"plied *Maria* laughing). You had bet-
"ter, my dear Papa, confider on this
"matter, or a trip to *Scotland* may be
"the confequence; for though the
"good doctor is of age, yet as I am
"hardly eighteen, I cannot difpofe of
"myfelf without your confent."

Never was an evening more agreeably paffed, or a company more delighted with each other. Mr. *Coventry*'s fpirits, though never in the higheft
key, may be called fweetly in tune;

not

not unlike that kind of harmony, which gently vibrates on the ear, and never fails to lull the mind into a pleafing calm, without raifing thofe lively ideas which are infpired by more fprightly notes.

THE doctor was propofing a party at whift, when a fervant entered with a letter, which juft then came from the Office.

" LORD *L——!*" faid Mr. *Coventry,* looking at the fuperfcription.

THE doctor, who had laid afide his pipe to engage at cards, now relighted it, and the Ladies in a low voice were talking of their next day's excurfion, when Mr. *Coventry* having perufed the letter gave it to his daughter, faying, " Lord *L——*, my dear, has given ' us a new relatio n."

" Not a wife, I hope," cried doctor *Edgcome*, throwing down his pipe;
and being anſwered in the affirmative,
" If that is the caſe, (continued he)
" even I cannot be ſafe; for ſince that
" knave *Cupid* has with his feathers
" tickled the heart of a batchelor of
" fifty-five, may not fourſcore be in
" equal danger ?—I proteſt, my little
" cherub, (to *Maria*) this piece of
" news has amazingly diſcompoſed me !
" Well, I believe I muſt run from you
" at laſt."

" Supposing I tell you, friend, (ſaid
" Mr. *Coventry*, ſmiling at his humour)
" that Lord *L——* never intended to
" live a batchelor, and has been long
" enaged to the Lady he now married,
" their union only delayed from family
" reaſons."

G 5 " I am

" I AM fatisfied, (he replied) and
" now will venture to afk what kind
" of woman he has made choice of."

" ONE (returned Mr. *Coventry*)
" every way calculated to make him
" happy.—What think you of the ami-
" able Lady *Mary Haftings?*"

" I AM not acquainted with her
" Ladyfhip (anfwered the doctor); but
" common Fame, I know, has been
" very loud in her praifes."

" COMMON Fame (faid Mr. *Coven-*
" *try*) is called a common Liar: but
" you fhall be a judge if fhe has not
" told truth in regard to Lady *Mary.*
" I expect her Ladyfhip with her Lord
" next week: their coming will make
" me vaftly happy, as my dear child
" confines herfelf too much with me."

" O SAY

"O say not this," cried the amiable *Maria*, who had juft then finifhed reading the letter: "Was I to devote "every hour, nay every minute of "my life, would it be too much for "fuch a father?"

"My deareft child, (faid the en-"raptured parent, hugging her to his "breaft) fuch duty and goodnefs were "certainly fent to compenfate for the "lofs of thy bleffed mother."

Doctor *Edgcome* not approving the turn this converfation feemed likely to take, prudently gave it another, by afking if Lord and Lady *L——* brought any company with them.

Mr. *Coventry* replied, that Mr. *Stormont* and Mifs *Haftings* were propofed of the party; the former a ward of

his

his Lordſhip, the latter related to his Lady.

"Mr. *Stormont!* (ſaid the doctor) "I fancy I was acquainted with his "father. Can you tell me if his fa‑ "mily are of *Worceſter?*"

BEING anſwered affirmatively, "I "know nothing (purſued he) of this "young branch, but will aver the old "ſtock is as good and honeſt as any in "the kingdom. Nay, let me tell my "Primroſe and Daffodil, they muſt "keep a ſtrict guard at the door of "their hearts: ſhould he be half ſo "handſome as his father, they will "elſe play them a runaway trick."

BOTH Ladies promiſing to take his advice, the converſation continued chearful and entertaining till that hour

arrived

arrived at which they retired for the night.

MISS *Coventry* and *Lavinia* being now at liberty to chat with freedom, began to talk over the occurrences of the paſſed day, and again wiſhed for the hour which was to carry them to the Woods.

HERE I will ſuppoſe my reader, eſpecially if a female, not to be ſo void of curioſity as to regret my paſſing over the neceſſary orders given by Miſs *Coventry* for the reception of her noble relations; a morning-viſit from Miſs *Jones's*, or their thouſand profeſſions of friendſhip to *Maria*; in order to bring that Lady and Miſs *Gilford* once more to the place of rendezvous.

BEING

BEING arrived at the narrow lane, Mifs *Coventry* ordered the fervants to wait, as they had done the preceding day; and entering the woods found there the venerable Sage, leaning on a ftaff, and fo deeply buried in contemplation, that he never lifted his eyes from the ground, or knew any thing of their approach, till they fpoke, which roufed him from his revèrie.

AFTER anfwering their inquiries for his health, he faid they were very punctual to their appointment.

" WE would not have made you " wait, Sir, (replied *Lavinia*) for the " univerfe; but we are not to ftay " here: you laft night was fo good to " fay, you would conduct us to your " houfe."

" To

" To my houſe! (he repeated) Yes,
" ſo I will; but you muſt not expect,
" my children, the edifice noble, rooms
" lofty, or fretted roofs : yet he who
" built it can, at his own pleaſure,
" make even the meaneſt cot more deſi-
" rable than the moſt ſplendid palace."

Hᴀᴠɪɴɢ ſaid this, he led them
through ſeveral intricate paths, and
at length ſtruck into one ſo extremely
narrow, as made it difficult to paſs,
the end of which they did not gain
for many minutes, and were then un-
utterably ſurpriſed to find it terminate
in a rock : nor could they perceive any
way by which to proceed. They
looked on each other, and for the firſt
time began to entertain thoughts not in
favour of their conductor, which were
ſtrengthened by his obſerving a ſtrict
ſilence.

Wʜᴀᴛ

WHAT would they have now given to have been at *Weatly*! blaming themfelves, no doubt, for having rafhly ventured to fo retired a place with a perfon they had never feen but once before.   His venerable afpect, that goodnefs which they imagined fo confpicuous in every look and word, fhould not, ought not, to have been fo much relied on:—Appearances often deceive: —How eafy for a villain to put on the mafk of virtue !

UNABLE to communicate their dreadful apprehenfions to each other, they were finking with fear, when the perfon who raifed it taking a key from his pocket, applied it to the rock, which opened, as if by enchantment, fufficient for two to enter.   " O my God! " (cried *Maria* in a low voice) what " is to become of us !"

" LET

" LET us rely on Heaven," whifpered
Mifs *Gilford.* She could add no more:
the ftranger offered her his hand,
faying he would return in an inftant
and fetch her friend.

LAVINIA knew that refiftance could
be of no fervice: they were now too
much in his power, and even to fhew
a diftruft would be impolitic; for
which reafon fhe fuffered him to lead
her, though with trembling fteps.

MISS *Coventry* faw her enter the
dreadful cavern ! What at that moment was her emotion! Affrighted,
terrified, fhe looked on every fide to
fee if there was no way to efcape ; but
none appeared, except the little path
by which they came; the wood being
fo thick on either hand, that it was abfolutely impoffible to penetrate it. She
had

had once thoughts of trying the fwift-
nefs of her feet, nay, had actually re-
tracted fome fteps, when the voice of
Friendfhip bid her return. " Could
" fhe leave (it afked) in that fhocking
" place her dear *Lavinia?*" This
fingle queftion determined her; fhe
came back, refolved to fhare the fame
fate with her friend, and offered up a
fervent prayer to the Almighty for his
protection. The petition came from
a heart too pure to be rejected. Whilft
her lovely eyes were looking to that
heaven from whence fhe expected
fuccour, half her fears vanifhed; and
when the old gentleman again ap-
proached her, fhe did not feel thofe
perturbations fhe had done a few minutes fince.

" COME, my child, (faid he, with
" ineffable benignity) condefcend to
" enter

" enter my humble cell.   This is my
" houfe. I bad you not expect a lofty
" dome.   The head of Ambition has
" never yet entered my dwelling.   Be-
" lieve me, Madam, the parade and
" buftle we muft neceffarily meet in
" the world, though ever fo fortunate,
" cannot compenfate for the tranquil
" eafe I here enjoy."

MISS *Coventry*, who had now loft
fight of every fear, liftened whilft he
fpoke with reverential pleafure; and
by his affiftance reached the laft of
about twenty fteps, that were either
worn by Time, or hewn by Art, to an
eafy declivity, which led to a fmall
neat room, whofe craggy fides were
covered with the bark of trees, floored
with the fame materials.

A COUCH,

A COUCH, three chairs, a little table and a book-cafe, compleated the furniture.

HERE the Ladies were again re-united; they gazed on each other with aftonifhment; they appeared to wonder; but their furprife was unattended by fufpicion.

As foon as the Hermit had feated his fair guefts, he prefented them with cake and fweet-meats; nor was a glafs of excellent Madeira, which he infifted on their drinking, at all unfeafonable, having lately fuffered fo much from their timidity : but with all their engaging rhetoric, they could not prevail on their abftemious hoft to tafte the wine.

" I WOULD

" I would oblige you, (faid he)
" was it in my power; but that is an
" indulgence I never allow myfelf, un-
" lefs my health or fpirits abfolutely
" require it, which is not now the
" cafe : on the contrary, my heart feels
" a lightnefs to which it has been long
" unaccuftomed."

" Pardon me, my dear young
" Lady, (to *Lavinia*) I find myfelf
" ftrangely impatient for the fequel of
" your pretty narrative. I intreat you
" will remove the cloud which feems
" to hang over the conduct of your
" lover. Methinks I am interefted in
" his favour. To me he appears de-
" ferving. He muft not, cannot be
" unamiable."

Miss *Gilford's* eyes fparkled the
approbation of her foul, at the praifes
given

given Mr. *Gore* by this good old man ;
and without waiting to be folicited a
fecond time, fhe began to fatisfy his
curiofity in the following manner.

CHAP. XII.

" **I** LEFT off yefterday at my receiv-
"   ing a letter from Mr. *Gore* by the
" hands of *Sally* ; the contents fo un-
" expected, and I then thought fo ex-
" tremely cruel, thatI will not attempt
" to tell you what I felt on this occa-
" fion.   I fuppreffed my tears be-
" fore my mother and brother : but
" when alone, they were my only con-
" folation.

" I OFTEN

" I often afked *Sally* if fhe had
" heard nothing of Mr. *Gore*; which
" fhe was fure to anfwer in the nega-
" tive.   Indeed, I have fince wondered
" at my blindnefs: the leaft penetra-
" tion might have difcovered that fhe
" was now more in Sir *William*'s in-
" tereft than in mine: but my eyes
" were not open to her bafenefs, till
" her own confcience could no longer
" keep the horrid fecret.

" One evening my fpirits being ex-
" tremely low, I went to my room
" as foon as the cloth was removed;
" and taking up a volume of *Shake-*
" *fpear*, I opened it to his excellent
" play intitled *Much Ado about No-*
" *thing*.

" Hero's diftrefs affected me: I
" wept as I read it.—*Sally*, who I had
" em-

" employed about fome work of which
" I was grown tired, begged I would
" put down my book : " I am fure,
" Madam, (faid fhe) it muft be a mife-
" rable melancholy one to make you
" cry fo. I could never in my born
" days endure to read ftories of ghofts
" and murders ; they fo befrighten
" me, that for all the good in the
" world I fhould fee them when I go
" to bed."

" SMILING at her ignorant fimpli-
" city, I replied, " It is neither one
" or the other, Sally ; yet it affects
" me more than if I had read a relation
" of all the ghofts that have appeared
" the laft hundred years."

" LORD, Madam ! (faid fhe) if it
" would not be making too bold, I
" fhould furely afk what it was about."

" THINK-

" THINKING no more than juſt to
" amuſe myſelf with the remarks of
" ſuch a perſon, I began to relate the
" heads of what I had been reading,
" to which I obſerved ſhe liſtened
" with great attention, and really
" made ſome judicious remarks on
" the whimſical characters of *Benedict*
" and *Beatrice :* but when I came to
" that part where *Margaret* is pitched
" on by Don *John* to repreſent *Hero*
" to the deceived *Claudio*, a death-
" like paleneſs overſpread her face,
" the work dropped from her hand,
" and ſhe cried out with eyes ſtaring
" as if ſhe had really ſeen a ſpectre,
" I am guilty ! You have diſcovered
" me, Madam ! I cannot hope for
" your forgiveneſs !" and down ſhe
" fell on her knees before me.

" WHAT is the matter ! (exclaim-
" ed I) what ails the girl?" though in-
" deed I was scarce ever more terrified.

" THE matter, Miss *Lavinia !* (said
" the conscious wretch, sobbing) To
" be sure you know it already, or could
" never have told my wicked plot to
" deceive Mr. *Gore.* Aye, aye, Ma-
" dam, I knew who you meant by
" *Margaret."*

" GOOD God! I shuddered with hor-
" ror and amazement ; but perceiving
" I must owe her confession to a sup-
" position that I was before acquainted
" with her crimes, I bad her in a stern
" voice get up, and if she hoped for
" my pardon to tell me every particular
" of her business, and who it was that
" made her commit so black a trans-
" action.

" AH !

" Ah! what a fcene of iniquity
" had fhe to difclofe! I fhall faulter
" in a repetition."

" PROCEED, my dear child," faid
the Sage. An affenting nod prevented the fame requeft from Mifs
Coventry.

" I WAS obliged (continued *Lavi-*
" *nia*) to repeat my commands feveral
" times before I could get her from
" her knees: fhe then trembled fo as
" to be forced to fupport herfelf a-
" gainft the back of a chair.

" I AM ignorant, Madam, (faid the
" agitated creature) who can have be-
" trayed me to you; but this I am fure,
" I have never had my right mind fince
" Sir *William More* overcame my
" honefty."

" WHAT!

" WHAT ! (cried I, not mifunder-
" ftanding her words, but as it feems
" mifapplying them) poor wretch !
" haft thou then fallen a victim to that
" vileft of men ! O *Sally, Sally!* and
" Sir *William More* has really feduced
" thee ! This I did not know before."

" GOD be thanked ! God be thank-
" ed ! (replied fhe fobbing) I ben't
" what I believe you take me to be,
" Madam.   No, no, I have preferved
" my *vartue* ; though I did, I did, I
" did, to be fure, lofe my name, when
" I confented to betray and ruin fo
" fweet a young Lady."

" A MINUTE fince I trembled for
" the poor wretch : now every fear re-
" doubled on my own account.

" SPEAK,

" SPEAK, (cried I) explain yourſelf;
" but firſt reach me ſome water." She
" tottered to the ſtand, and bringing
" me the bottle, I ſwallowed a mouth-
" full, which probably kept me from
" fainting.   " Now (ſaid I) go on,
" conceal nothing from me, and per-
" haps I may forgive you."

" I COULD not prevent her from
" again falling on her knees, to bleſs
" me for what I had half promiſed;
" and I really believe ſhe was a very
" ſincere penitent.

" SEEING my impatience, and be-
" ing often ordered to riſe, ſhe reſumed
" her place at the back of my chair,
" and proceeded thus:

" You may remember, Madam,
" that the laſt afternoon you ever ſent

H 3   " me

" me to Mr. *Willace*'s, I brought back
" a letter from Mr. *Gore*, which made
" you very ill ; and I thought then, if fo
" be as how I fhould have the whole
" *univarfe* to do you harm, I would
" not have earned it : but alackaday !
" I verily believe *James* muft have
" given love-powder to bewitch me,
" or I fhould never have turned about
" to be of another mind. To be fure,
" Madam, I had a little kindnefs for
" Mr. *James* ; but never thought as
" how he had any for me, becaufe he
" was very often kiffing *Sufan* the
" dairy-maid, and fhe made her brags
" all about that he was her fweet-
" heart."

" PRITHEE, girl, (faid I) teize me
" no longer with affairs of which I
" want not to be informed."

" MY

" My dear Lady, pray fuffer me to
" fpeak for myfelf (replied fhe), or
" you will mayhap think me more
" *bafer* than I am."

" I FOUND fhe would go on in her
" own way, fo I bid her proceed.

" The night you was taken ill,
" Mr. *James*, after I had put my
" Lady to bed, brought me a letter:
" at the fame time he told me as how,
" Don't be a fool, my dear *Sally*; I
" love you better than any earthly crea-
" ture: but we can never marry ti'l
" we have got a little money before-
" hand; therefore you muft do as his
" Honour defires."

" To be fure I was glad to hear him
" fpeak fo kindly; but before I could
" afk him if he meant me true, he

H 4 " was

" was gone out of the room ; and,
" God be thanked! being brought
" pretty well to my pen, I opened the
" letter he left, and was quite bewil-
" dered to find it come from fo great a
" gentleman as Sir *William*.

" I READ it over and over, and at
" laft underftood that if I would fet
" out and come to him directly, he
" would make it worth my while.
" So when I came to this part, I faid
" to myfelf, I would not go on any
" confideration, as his Honour could
" not want me for good : but reading
" and reading on, I found he did not
" intend me any hurt, becaufe he faid
" as how he knew Mr. *James* was my
" fweet-heart, and had defired him to
" come along with me, becaufe I
" fhould not have any doubts about
" my *vartue*."

" So

" So you went (said I) at this sum-
" mons, did you, *Sally ?*"

" INDEED, indeed, I resolved not
" to go, Madam; *for why*, I knew
" you thought his Honour a very bad
" man : but Mr. *James* coming just
" then was very angry, and said as
" how if that was the cafe, and I
" would not go, he would give my
" Lady warning the next day.

" WHAT could I do, Madam ?—
" What could I do? (said the weeping
" criminal) If *James* had gone away,
" I should never have had a minute's
" heart's ease afterwards : so I did—I
" did—I did tell him, that if so be
" as how he would not give warning,
" I would go."

" WELL, and you did go ?"

" YES,

"YES, Madam, I cannot fay but I
"did."

"LORD help me! (faid I) but
"proceed; and again I charge you,
"hide nothing from me.

"I HELD by *James* all the way.
"As you chufe, Madam, to have me
"particular, upon my word, and in-
"deed, I will be very particular.
"Yet though Mr. *James* was with me,
"and I held by his arm, I fhook
"all over with fear; and every now
"and then fancied I faw *ghoftes's*, tho'
"I fuppofe there is no fuch things in
"thefe parts. And though it is but
"a fhort mile to Sir *William*'s houfe, I
"thought as how the road grew longer
"and longer, and was ready to die
"when *James* let me in through the
"great gate."

"HIS

" His Honour was fitting at a ta-
" ble fpread all over with golden gui-
" neas.

" Though I was but a fervant he
" got up, and was fo good-humoured
" as to kifs me, and fhook my fweet-
" heart by the hand, faying, whilft
" we bowed and curtfied, " I am glad
" to fee you, Mr. *James,* efpecially
" as you have brought your pretty
" *Sally* with you ;" and his Honour
" fwore we were a comely couple,
" and then was fo kind to fay he would
" ftand up for our firft boy.

" I wish, (faid *James,* whilft I to
" be fure, Madam, was quite daunted,
" and blufhed like any thing) I wifh
" it was come to that: but your Wor-
" fhip muft know I am but a poor
" man, and *farvice* is no inheritance:
" and

" and tho' I love *Sally* as my life, yet
" before we marry, I am afraid I
" fhall be forced to accept of the offer
" Squire *Jones* made me yefterday."

" What was that?" afked his
Honour.

" It was (faid *James*) to go to *An-*
" *tigua* for ten years, for which I am
" to have five hundred pounds."

" O my dear injured Lady! (con-
" tinued the poor creature) I thought
" thofe dreadful words would have
" been my death : indeed, I could not
" help crying, though I hid it with
" my apron, which Sir *William* took
" from my face, and faid, " Indeed,
" *James*, you are to blame to let fuch
" pretty eyes weep for you."

" James

" JAMES wiped his eyes too, and
" faid he wifhed as how he could help
" it.

" COME, come, (cried his Honour)
" let us try, Mrs. *Sally*, if you and I
" can prevent honeft *James* from go-
" ing over fea. Now tell me, child,
" what would you do to keep him at
" home ; and, what is more, marry
" and live comfortably with him?"

" I SAID, I faid, I cannot deny it,
" Madam, I faid I would do any thing
" in my power ; for I thought as how
" I already faw him on the cruel
" ocean.

" WELL, then, it is in your power
" to keep him always with you (faid
" his Honour, taking one of my hands,
" whilft *James* held the other) ; and
" this

" this gold (pointing to the table) is all
" your own, my girl, if you will affift
" me in a good turn."

" OH heaven! (cried I) Take care,
" take care, *Sally*, that you repeat
" every word this vile Sir *William* faid,
" when he told the black affair you
" was to execute."

" ALL this time the creature wept
" very plentifully, and wiping her
" eyes told me, fhe had not forgot a
" word his Honour had faid, and would
" tell me juft as he fpoke them.

" SALLY, (faid he) you know I am
" very foon to marry your young Lady:
" you know too that *Gore* pretends to
" difpute her heart with me. Now by
" fome means or other he has difco-
" vered that *Thurfday* is fixed upon by
" Lady

" Lady *Gilford* and Sir *Francis* for my
" nuptials with *Lavinia*, and this af-
" ternoon he fent for me. " Kill," or
" be killed," was the word.   Having
" no inclination to either, I would have
" argued the cafe ; but as nothing
" would content the fellow, I was
" forced to forge an inftant falfhood.
" I faid, Mifs *Gilford* was not worth
" our fwords or refentment, and that
" laft evening I difcovered her perfidy;
" that fhe had another lover, and ac-
" tually met him every night at a little
" window which looked into the
" grove."

   " O GOOD your Honour! (faid I)
" how could you fay fuch a thing ?
" Sure my Lady never met a Chriftian
" man in that place in her born days."

                        " I KNOW

"I KNOW it, *Sally* (replied he);
" but this is not now the matter. Tho'
" it was a long while before *Gore* would
" give the leaſt credit to my tale, he
" now begins to believe it; for I have
" abſolutely promiſed, that to-morrow-
" night at eleven, the time I told him
" when I was informed they generally
" met, his eyes, his ears, ſhould con-
" vince him how little worthy ſhe was
" of his or my regard. Now it re-
" mains on you, *Sally*, to help me to
" fulfil this engagement. At the time
" and place appointed do you be there,
" dreſſed in your Lady's crimſon hat
" and cloak: lean out at the window;
" *James* ſhall be under; but ſpeak
" low, that your voice may not be dif-
" covered. He will ſay to you, " My
" deareſt Miſs *Gilford*, why am I not
" in a rank of life to appear openly
                                    " your

" your lover ?"—Then anfwer him,
" that you would prefer him to a
" prince, even if he was ten times
" meaner than he is. Say, that you
" pretend a paffion for *Gore* only to
" hide your love to him ; and fay alfo,
" you hate, you defpife me. Call me
" a villain, or any other bad name ;
" but be fure, *Sally*, you do not for-
" get to fpeak all this extremely foft.",

C H A P,

CHAP. XIII.

HERE *Lavinia* was interrupted by a voice which exclaimed, " Vile! inexorable! plotting villain!" At the same time a man of about five-and-twenty appeared before them, and flung himself at the feet of Mifs *Gilford*, who, as foon as fhe heard, or rather faw him, gave a violent fcream, and fell to the ground.

MARIA, though terrified almoft to a degree of frenzy, flew to fupport her fallen lifelefs friend: but fhe was already in the arms of him who had occafioned this diforder. He wept over her; he intreated, as if fhe ftill heard him,

him, that fhe would live; that fhe
would forgive his weak credulity.——
Thefe and fome other words to the
fame effect convinced Mifs *Coventry*,
the perfon whom fhe now faw was the
identical Mr. *Gore*.

His eyes exprefled generofity, fenfibility, tendernefs : the laft all fhow-
ered on *Lavinia*, who was by this
time laid upon the couch, and fo much
recovered as to be able to blefs her
tranfported lover with fo fweet a look,
as would have repayed him for ten
years of anguifh.

As for the old gentleman, he rub-
bed his hands, ftroked his beard, and
once more produced that fame bottle of
Madeira which made its appearance in
a former chapter.

" Come,

"Come, my children, (faid the
"good man) after the fright my ne-
"phew has occafioned you, another
"glafs will be abfolutely neceffary."

"Your nephew! Mr. *Gore* your
"nephew! (repeated *Lavinia*) Hea-
"ven and earth! what new wonders!
"Certainly (cried Mifs *Coventry*) we
"are tranfported into Fairy land': every
"thing we hear and fee is ftrange and
"furprifing."

"Indeed, my dear Mifs *Gilford*,
"(faid Mr. *Gore*) this venerable, this
"good man is my uncle. It is to him
"I am indebted for every fentiment
"deferving approbation. It is by his
"advice that I have been with-held
"from many actions which would
"have given me pain, when I came to
"reflect on them; yet there is one
"debt

" debt greater than the reft, which I
" mention laft : It is to him I owe my
" prefent happinefs. Had it not been for
" him, I fhould ftill have thought you
" falfe, blinded by the *Machiavelian*
" art of a curfed contriver; but Sir
" *William More* ftill lives."

" And ftill fhall live, if his God
" permit (interrupted the uncle of
" Mr. *Gore*): but we will talk on this
" topick fome other time.—You broke
" in upon us, young gentleman, at a
" very interefting part of Mifs *Gilford's*
" narrative, nor will I pardon you,
" unlefs you prevail on her to proceed."

" I fear, Sir, (faid Mr. *Gore*) her
" fpirits are too much weakened by
" the late fhock they have fuftained ;
" but with Mifs *Gilford's* permiffion,
" though it will be greatly to your dif-
" advan-

" advantage, I will fatisfy you as far
" as is in my power. This propofal
" met a general approbation ; *Lavinia*
" in particular feemed highly pleafed.

" IT has already appeared but too
" plain (faid he) that *Sally* could not
" withftand the united powers of love
" and affluence ; it is certain fhe did
" not by what followed ; for at the fixed
" time Sir *William* called on me, and
" we went to the place appointed,
" where I thought I faw the beft, the
" moft deferving of her fex changed
" into a falfe, perfidious ingrate. I
" heard the very words which *Sally* re-
" peated to her Lady ; I faw the wretch
" lean forward to her accomplice ; and
" my tranfports of rage were fo un-
" governable, that I would have fal-
" len inftantly on my fuppofed rival, if
" his vile employer, who I now regard-
" ed

" ed as my beſt friend, had not with-
" held me.

" W<small>HAT</small> can I ſay in defence of
" my ſtupidity? only that I was blind-
" ed by infatuation, and that the glim-
" mering light from a moon in its de-
" cline helped to deceive me.

" A<small>FTER</small> ſuppoſing myſelf con-
" vinced of your perfidy, I was impa-
" tient to leave the hated ſpot; Let us
" (ſaid I) let us go from this falſe, this
" fickle woman, whom I now deſpiſe."

" S<small>IR</small> *William* ſaid every thing he
" could deviſe to heighten my jealouſy,
" if that had been poſſible.

" W<small>E</small> returned together to Mr.
" *Willace*, who was ſhocked at the al-
" teration a few hours had made in
" me.——

" me.—He begged to know the caufe.
" I refufed to fatisfy him, ftill anxious
" for the reputation of one I had once
" fo truly, fo ardently loved; whom
" yet I could not avoid loving.   I even
" made Sir *William*, who had folemn-
" ly affured me he would never ad-
" drefs Mifs *Gilford*, as folemnly pro-
" mife to keep her folly a fecret.

" UNABLE to ftay at *Weatly*, where
" I was every day fubject to fee my
" ftill dear, and as I thought falfe, *La-*
" *vinia*, I took my leave of Mr. *Wil-*
" *lace*, firft fending a note not to up-
" braid Mifs *Gilford*, but to let her
" know I was no ftranger to her infi-
" delity.

" ON my going from *Weatly*, I had
" fome thoughts of proceeding to *Lon-*
" *don*; but changed them in favour of
                                    " my

" my own houfe, about three miles
" from this place, which I preferred
" for the fatisfaction of feeing and re-
" ceiving advice and confolation from
" the beft of men.

" NOTWITHSTANDING my uncle
" did and faid every thing to make me
" conquer a paffion which appeared to
" be fo ill placed, yet he found it a tafk
" not to be accomplifhed : your idea
" followed me every where.

" IT is impoffible to fay what I felt
" when my uncle this morning related
" to me his interview with you the
" preceding evening ; but how were
" my tranfports encreafed, upon being
" told I fhould fee you in a few hours.
" My revered director thought I had
" beft conceal myfelf, where I could
" hear the remainder of your ftory. I

" mitted; you came; I faw you enter,
" and felt emotions fuch as cannot be
" defcribed.

" Oh! I could for ever have liftened
" to the mufic of your voice, had you
" not fixed my whole attention on the
" villainy of that detefted wretch, who
" had poifoned my foul with fufpi-
" cion. You fhewed me what a fool,
" what a dupe, I had been. I could
" not fupprefs a fudden guft of paffion.
" My abrupt appearance was the con-
" fequence, by which my deareft *La-*
" *vinia* and her charming friend were
" fo greatly terrified. And now, ma-
" dam (taking the hand of his amiable
" miftrefs, with eyes expreffing the
" very foul of contrition), will you, can
" you forgive a crime unpremeditated?
" **Can you** forget that I have contami-
                              " nated

" nated the purity of your mind with
" dark, injurious fufpicions?"

" INDEED (faid Mifs *Gilford*, in the
" fweeteft voice imaginable) I ought
" not to forgive you; for had I not
" ftood on a very tottering bafis, fuch
" a wretch as Sir *William More* would
" not fo eafily have pufhed me from
" your good opinion: yet his uncom-
" mon arts muft, I think, plead in
" your favour."

" EXALTED goodnefs! (replied Mr.
" *Gore)* every hour of my life will be
" too little———"

" STOP, Sir (interrupting him) your
" pardon is not yet paffed my lips,
" though I can affure you it has long
" been made out in my heart. Com-
" ply with one requeft, and———"

I 2   " OH

" Oh name it, my beloved Mifs
" *Gilford* (cried Mr. *Gore*), and hate
" me if I deny it."

" Pray, Sir (faid *Maria*) will you
" pardon me if I prefume to make
" another ?"

" You do me honour, madam,"
faid he.

" Well, but firft (continued Mifs
" *Coventry*) let *Lavinia* make her's ;
" and, as her friend, I fhall afterwards
" venture to deliver mine."

" I will then ; and remember, Sir,
" you bad me hate you, if I find my
" boon difregarded.   Promife me that
" you will never challenge the worft
" of men, and that no behaviour of
" his fhall ever make you forget that
" promife."

" What

" WHAT hard conditions!" replied
Mr. *Gore*.

" SUCH as you fhould accept with
" pleafure (interrupted his venerable
" uncle); and fuch as your heart ought
" to have fuggefted, had this lady
" never mentioned them."

" BUT what will the world fay,
" fhould I let him go unpunifhed?
" You know, my dear Sir, I am paf-
" fionate : how then can I rein in my
" juft refentment ?"

" I WILL put you in a way to com-
" mand it (returned he), if you liften
" to my advice. In the place of re-
" fentment fubftitute pity : look on
" him as below the former, and only
" worthy of the latter, as he is a fellow-
" creature, ftamped with the image of
I 3 " his

" his Divine Creator, though he has fo
" vilely debafed it.   Let this one con-
" fideration inftantly banifh   every
" thought of revenge : for if his God,
" whom   he   has   much   higher of-
" fended, permits him to live, perhaps
" to repent, fhall you try to fhorten
" thofe days his goodnefs has allowed
" him ?   Reflect a moment : in that
" moment fuppofe this miferable crea-
" ture, at the laft day, upbraiding you
" for thofe torments denounced againft
" him : But for you, he will then fay,
" I might now have been happy ; you
" cut me off when my fins were at
" the higheft."

" I own all you fay, Sir (replied
" Mr. *Gore)* to be extremely juft; but
" fhould fuch a man, for fuch a crime,
" go unpunifhed, what next may he
" not attempt ? Shall none revenge
                                    " the

" the wrongs of thofe he renders mi-
" ferable?"

" YES (returned the fage), there is
" one, and only one, who has a right
" to do it.

" HAS any perfon a greater (faid
" Mr. *Gore*, colouring) than myfelf?
" Prove but this, and I fwear from
" that inftant his life fhall be fafe as
" the deareft of my friends."

" AGREED (cried the elder Mr.
" *Gore*). Thofe ladies (addrefling *La-*
" *vinia* and *Maria*) fhall be our um-
" pires. How, young gentleman, ap-
" ply you thofe words, *Vengeance is*
" *mine, fays the Lord, and I will re-*
" *pay it.*"

" I

" I WILL not (faid his nephew,
" with the moſt ineffable grace) aſk
" to hear the deciſion of our fair
" judges, but confefs myſelf con-
" vinced, and that I ſhould have done
" a very unwarrantable action. Here
" then I ſincerely promiſe my dear
" *Lavinia*, and you, Sir, never to pur-
" ſue Sir *William* with a thought of
" revenge."

MISS *Gilford* both by words and
looks expreffed the joy this declaration gave her ; every feature appeared
newly animated ; the roſe, which had
been for ſome months faded, ſeemed
at this inſtant to receive a ſecond
birth ; it ſprang up ſpontaneous ; the
beauteous glow and infant ſweet-
nefs of the bud ſpoke in her bluſh-
ing cheek.

MR.

MR. *Gore*'s pleasure is only to be supposed by those in a similar situation; his uncle's was not less exquisite, tho' more serene and tranquil; whilst Miss *Coventry*'s was little inferior to either, seeing the friend she loved so unexpectedly restored to the man her heart approved.

LAVINIA's curiosity was lulled asleep by the presence of her lover; but it was not the same with *Maria*, who now reminded Mr. *Gore*, he had not yet granted her request, nor permitted her to make it.

HE asked her pardon, and said she need only mention her commands to have them instantly obeyed.

" I DARE not command (replied she, " with an air of the utmost sprightli-
I 5   " ness)

" nefs); I am the humbleft fuppliant
" in the world, and fue for your inte-
" reft with this moft revered of men,
" that he will condefcend to tell us
" why he flies from fociety? why he
" buries himfelf in this fubterraneous
" dwelling?"

" My dearest child (replied the
" elder Mr. *Gore*), you fhall not need
" my nephew's interceffion; I am
" ready to fatisfy your curiofity, after I
" have led you through my little ha-
" bitation."

Lavinia's lover having defired the
honour of her hand, " Come, my
" good young lady (continued he), will
" you accept the hand of an old
" man?" to *Maria*.

" Gladly,

" GLADLY, Sir (she replied); and
" with the fame confidence I would
" my father's. Indeed, your fenti-
" ments are fo like my dear parent's,
" that I cannot help looking on you
" with reverential duty."

" HARRY (faid he, applying to his
" nephew), could you have thought
" vanity would have found its way to
" this humble rock? But I now find
" walls of flint will not exclude it.
" Look round, my charming gueft :
" what fee you here to make me vain?
" yet I feel I really am fo ; nay, per-
" haps more, and with greater caufe,
" than a monarch on his throne. Has
" not this deferving young creature
" (faid he) regarded me with duty? But
" fay, my fweet child, will you per-
" mit me to love you with a father's
" fondnefs ?"

I 6   " WILL.

" WILL I (repeated the delighted
" *Maria)* ! O Heavens, how you op-
" prefs me with goodnefs! My dear,
" dear Sir, from this hour look on me
" with a paternal eye. How happy
" in two fuch parents!"

" CHARMING excellence (wiping
" away the tears that fell on his fur-
" rowed cheek)! Yes, you are, you
" fhall be my adopted daughter. Yet,
" alas! I have no inheritance to be-
" queath you: all my poffeffions are
" forrows."

" AH, my dear father, deny me not
" a child's part; give me a portion out
" of thofe forrows. This I entreat the
" more, as I have really none of my
" own."

" GRACIOUS

" GRACIOUS Heaven (replied the
" fage) has at laft looked on me with
" a pitying eye : it fends me another
" child : again I am a father. And
" you will fometimes, my deareft *Ma-*
" *ria,* vifit me ? Your natural parent
" would not deny me to fhare with him
" this comfort, did he know how I
" have been deprived of every other."

MISS *Coventry* replied, there fhould
pafs but few days in which fhe would
not vifit him, and petition his blefling.

C H A P.

C H A P. XIV.

HERE they were joined by *Lavinia* and Mr. *Gore.* The latter, feeing Mifs *Coventry* and his uncle engaged in converfation, had gently drawn the object of his wifhes to the farther end of the cell, and there whifpered a thoufand vows of conftancy, far from difpleafing to his fair miftrefs, if her countenance correfponded with her heart.

THEY now quitted the firft apartment, by a door which the ladies had not before perceived, each of their conductors a candle in his hand; a caution abfolutely neceffary, as this

cavity

cavity had no light like the outer room, to which it was conveyed by a fky-light fo curioufly contrived, as not to be vifible on the outfide.

AFTER proceeding about forty yards, they could plainly diftinguifh the found of waters; and exprefling their fur-prife, the elder Mr. *Gore* told them they were within twenty yards of a river; " the moft beautiful, perhaps, " (added he) in *Europe :* nay, I quef-" tion if my daughter and Mifs *Gil-*" *ford* will not, at firft, imagine they " are by fome magic conveyed to *Mex-*" *ico* or *Peru.*——But (continued he) let " me beg my dear children will in-" dulge an old man's requeft, and " fuffer me to lead them a few fteps " with their eyes blinded."

THEY

They confented to this propofal, and in lefs than a minute were told they might look about them.

Who can defcribe their aftonifhment to fee the roof, which was in the fhape of a dome, hung with ten thoufand fparkling gems: diamonds, emeralds, and rubies, appeared above, below, on every fide.—What ftill added to the amazing beauty of this place, was a tranfparent river, that ran on one fide, whofe clearnefs refembled chryftal.

Lavinia and *Maria* having exprefled their furprife and pleafure, began to examine more minutely thofe dazzling gems which met their fight.—
" Was ever any thing fo charming
" (faid Mifs *Coventry*) as that emerald
" crefcent!

" crefcent! It makes me wifh to be a
" follower of *Diana*, to have it placed
" upon my forehead."

" INDEED, it is very charming (re-
" plied Mifs *Gilford*); yet I confefs
" that diamond which reprefents a
" heart pleafes me infinitely more. But
" pray, gentlemen, (faid they both)
" fay by what *ignis fatuus* thefe things
" appear to us as they do?"

" You call this deception by a
" proper name (replied their venerable
" guide); it is an *ignis fatuus* that
" deceives you: a falfe light dazzles
" the opticks of your fight."

SAYING this he extinguifhed the
candles, and opening a fmall door,
the fun, which had been for two hours
excluded, again faluted them; but
fcarce

fcarce could its enlivening rays make a-
mends for the beautiful profpect that
vanifhed at its approach:—the diamonds, rubies, and emeralds were
now metamorphofed into congealed
drops, which by the nature of the
cavern petrified ere they could de-
fcend: the crefcent and heart were ftill
vifible, tho' no longer defirable orna-
ments.

The Ladies had not time given them
to make many reflections on this fudden and furprifing change; new beauties waited their attention: the profpect, indeed, was not extenfive, yet
every thing that could charm the fight,
or pleafe the imagination, feemed col-
lected into this one little fpot.

WHAT delighted them in a particular manner was the river, which
had

had its rife in the cavern, continued
through a fmall but beautiful plain,
where Nature had been lavifh of her
choiceft gifts.   To congratulate it on
leaving its dark prifon, flowers and
fhrubs were here planted by her hand
in fuch abundance, that it might not
improperly have been termed a wil-
dernefs of fweets.   Through thefe it
playfully wandered till a morofe wood,
envious of the happinefs of its fituation,
allured it to its gloomy abode, where
being once arrived, it was foon ob-
fcured from the fight.

THEIR fage Conductor having faftened the door through which they entered the plain, proceeded to a fmall
houfe, which the Ladies had not perceived, being planted thick on each
fide with trees.   As they came near,
they were met by a man of about fifty,
who

who was fo ftruck with feeing *Lavinia*
and Mifs *Coventry*, that for fome time
he could not utter a fyllable.

"Honest *Simon*, (faid Mr. *Gore*)
"we are come upon you a little ab-
"ruptly; but no matter: let us fee
"what the houfe affords. Come, is
"*Betty* within?"

"No, and pleafe your Honour,"
he replied, fomewhat recovered from
his furprife by the manner in which
his old mafter accofted him; "*Betty* is
"gone to the *Wink* to fill the tea-ket-
"tle; tho' it wants more than an hour
"of your Honour's ufual time."

"It does fo (faid the good Her-
"mit); but we are willing to fhew
"thefe Ladies we are not fo very fa-
"vage as our firft appearance befpoke
"us." This

THIS hint was enough for *Simon*, who, after making half a fcore bows to their ladyfhips, conducted them into a parlour: but without that appellation it might have been miftaken for a bower of jeffamines and woodbines, the walls being entirely covered with their luxuriant branches, which being now in full bloom, exhaled a fragrance hardly to be rivalled in either *India*.

MR. *Harry Gore* took a hand of each fair damfel, and feated them in a window which overlooked a parterre of flowers ending in a green flope, which ferved as a velvet margin to that river I have juft defcribed.

" WHAT a paradife, Mr. *Gore*
" (faid both Ladies), have you brought
" us to! Was ever any thing fo hea-
" venly! Ah (continued Mifs *Gil-*
" *ford*

" *ford* with inimitable fweetnefs)! one
" would think this day was deter-
" mined to make me remember it
" with pleafure to the end of my
" life."

THE entrance of his uncle did not
prevent this tranfported lover from
preffing to his faithful heart the hand
of his *Lavinia*.

MISS *Coventry*'s attention was now
engaged by a pretty playful fquirrel,
faftened by a fmall chain to the window; which the elder gentleman ob-
ferving, immediately giving freedom
to the little animal, prefented it to his
adopted daughter.

THIS prefent, though of no real value, yet as it came from the perfon
fhe revered next to her father, fhe received

ceived with delighted acknowledgements.

BETTY now entered with tea, followed by *Simon* with fruit, wine, and cakes; and as foon as the former was removed, the old gentleman did not wait to be reminded of giving them the particulars, which he doubted not had greatly raifed their curiofity, and addreffed them in the following words:

" I KNOW not, my dear children,
" what right I have to give you un-
" eafinefs; yet if you infift on the per-
" formance of my promife, I am now
" ready to fulfil it."

" BY no means would we requeft
" it (anfwered Mifs *Gilford*) if the re-
" cital will renew your grief."

" THAT it cannot do (he rejoin-
" ed); my unhappinefs is but too frefh
" in

" in my memory; it is ever before
" me; it is interwoven with my very
" exiftence; nor can I for a moment
" lofe fight of my forrows, till I
" am called to that place from
" whence they will be fhut out. I
" diftrefs you, Ladies! Wipe off thofe
" fympathetick drops, or I cannot
" think of proceeding."

THE fnowy cambrick, though not
more dazzling white than their com-
plexions, was now applied to their
eyes, by the affiftance of which the
heavenly azure and fparkling jet were
again reftored to their native luftre; and
Mr. *Gore* entered upon his hiftory, as
will be found in the next volume.

END of the FIRST VOLUME.

www.ingramcontent.com/pod-product-compliance
Lightning Source LLC
Chambersburg PA
CBHW030553040726
47497CB00008B/2710